SOMETHING DIFFERENT
OUT THERE

"When we go out into local space searching out worlds like ours we may be seeking out only those in a particular stage of immaturity, or maybe worlds that have become stuck in a kind of dead end. Maybe the places where the *real* pattern is—the places where the *real* story of life in the universe is being acted out—are places very different from this one. Our delusions may be just a cosmic joke. Maybe true alienness does exist at a level of intelligence we can't comprehend . . . and we can never come to terms with it; never reach it; never coexist with it; never be a part of it.

"The plan of life in the universe and its ultimate destiny is nothing whatsoever to do with *us*. There isn't any implication for human existence in anything I've said. Sometimes I think it might even do us good to see ourselves as others might see us, as we really might *be* in terms of the cosmos itself and its own history. As God might see us, if you like."

THE
PARADOX
OF
THE
SETS

Brian M. Stableford

DAW BOOKS, INC.
DONALD A. WOLLHEIM, PUBLISHER
New York

For Dave and Hazel Langford

FIRST PRINTING, OCTOBER 1979

1 2 3 4 5 6 7 8 9

DAW TRADEMARK REGISTERED
U.S. PAT. OFF. MARCA
REGISTRADA. HECHO EN U.S.A.

PRINTED IN U.S.A.

❋ 1 ❋

The chapter of accidents began as soon as it found the opportunity. We began signaling the planet as soon as we emerged into normal space and established a stable temporary orbit. We got a reply within minutes, breaking our previous record by a considerable margin. We couldn't believe that after a hundred and fifty years they'd have a man permanently stationed at the radio, and it seemed like a lucky accident that someone was passing by at the time. Accident it was, lucky it wasn't as things turned out.

The first person to respond to our call was a man who didn't give his name, probably because he was too busy wrestling with his astonishment. He had a bad case of buckpasser's disease and disappeared before we could establish meaningful communication in order to find someone more qualified to deal with unexpected emergencies. He was gone for some time, but he was eventually replaced by a woman who gave her name as Helene Levasseur. Her attitude was rather different—she seemed positively greedy for the opportunity to talk to us. She had a fast reaction time and she was a quick thinker. Right from the first moment she began to play her own game.

She didn't seem consumed with boundless joy when Nathan explained who we were and why we were visiting her world (which went by the unusually ugly name of Geb). We were used to that. After all, the colony had been here for a century and a half without Earth having bothered to send so much as a telegram of congratulation. She could be forgiven for a certain lack of enthusiasm on learning now that there was a ship circling up above carrying a crew of seven and offering to solve all the planet's problems with a cheery smile and a labfull of genetic engineering technology. We had learned to accept mild bitterness, strong sarcasm and even mild hostility, granting that there was some cause for any and all of them. A hundred and fifty years is a long time to be without a lifeline, or even a "hello." The colony had every right to believe that Earth had forgotten them or ignored them, and to resent that fact.

Despite her lack of joy, Helene Levasseur questioned us rapidly and efficiently on the purpose of our mission and the resources we had to help us carry it out. Nathan handled the answers with his customary charm, and the conversation was building up some momentum when Pete had to intervene to ask for instructions, suggestions or opinions on where he ought to land the ship.

The woman didn't seem to want to answer the question immediately. She broke the contact to talk to someone else, and when she came back it was with more questions about *Daedalus* and her equipment.

Pete got a little upset. He and Karen had had to make repairs on Attica, and he wasn't altogether happy about the condition of the ship. He wanted to get this last landing over—and he'd have been just as happy not to have to make it. He pressed for a decision, but Mme. Levasseur replied that it was a matter of putting the ship down where its resources could do most good. Geb, she said, was a big world, and its problems weren't gathered together in one corral.

It sounded reasonable enough, except for one thing. Even in a hundred and fifty years the colony shouldn't have expanded *that* much from the original landing site of the colony ships. But we were too pleased to be getting what sounded like a reasonable response to worry about quibbling.

Nathan asked politely for a decision, apologizing for the necessity of rushing her. She seemed reluctant—or made a show of seeming reluctant—and then she swooped.

"You have photographic equipment on board?" she asked.

"Yes," said Nathan, slightly peeved because he thought she was changing the subject again.

"Could you take some aerial photographs for us on your way in?"

Nathan looked up at Pete, showing his surprise but also asking a question. Pete frowned, and looked doubtful.

"That's a bit difficult," said Nathan. "It depends what you expect us to pick up with the pictures. You don't have to be too far up before you can't see anything at all. And then there's the matter of clouds. . . ."

The connection broke for another private conversation at the other end. Then she cut back in and said, "The weather's clear over the region we want scanned. Basically, what we want is for you to do a low pass over the mountain range in southeast Akhnaton. We can give you a landing site in the plain to the east. I'm in a small town about a hundred miles inland, but it doesn't matter if you overshoot me or fall short. Anywhere in the plain will do, provided that you could overpass the mountains as you come in and get the photographs."

"I don't think we can do that," said Nathan cautiously, still keeping one eye on Pete. He and Karen were looking at the map. Akhnaton was the largest continent, and the mountains were the biggest range on the planet—Geb's answer to the Himalayas, except they weren't quite so big and were close enough to the equator not to be so cold except on the peaks. The survey team had named them the Isis mountains. The only reason their leader had picked the world-name Geb was that it was the name of the Egyptian earth god, and it gave him *carte blanche* to name everything else that needed a name after something from ancient Egyptian history or mythology. It was a better way out of the problem than some I'd encountered.

"You say that you've come here to offer us help," said

Mme. Levasseur. "*Whatever help we need* was the way you phrased it, I believe. We need those pictures, and we don't have an airplane capable of taking them. The only way *we* can get up into the mountains is on donkey-back. But there's something we need to find that will show up from the air much better than from the ground."

"What?" asked Nathan. It sounded to me like a reasonable question.

"For the time being," she said, "I can't tell you. And to be quite honest, I'm not quite sure yet that we want you to know the story."

This time it was Nathan who broke the connection.

"They've got a bloody nerve," observed Karen.

"It's weird," I said. "Tell them we can't do it."

Nathan looked pensive, turning the matter over in his mind. "Can we?" he asked Pete.

Pete was still wearing the frown as if it had become permanent. Perhaps the wind had changed. "We'd take pictures as we came in anyhow," he said. "That's routine. Most of them need special analysis to yield any kind of data, but during the last couple of minutes we're low enough to spot objects on the ground—houses, cultivated fields."

"If there are houses and cultivated fields in those mountains," said Conrad, levelly, "then something's gone very wrong with their agricultural planning."

"It's a difficult flight-path," said Karen.

"But it's a possible one," admitted Pete. "If you think we ought to do it . . . the worst that can happen to us is atmospheric trouble and overheating in the systems. If we weren't near the end of the mission and the systems weren't a little dicey we could do it easily, but. . . ."

"If we can do it," said Nathan, "I think we ought to."

"Tell 'em to go to hell," offered Karen.

"That's not what we're here for," he reminded her.

"Then tell them to level with us. If they won't even

trust us to tell us what they want, why should we lean backwards to get it?"

"Because it's our job?" suggested Conrad.

"It's your decision, Pete," said Nathan. "But if it can be done safely, we have to do it. Anything that can gain us a little goodwill on the ground is necessary . . . and anything which has a negative effect is likely to make things very difficult."

"Okay," said Pete, without losing his frown. "I can do it. I'm sure."

Nathan switched on his microphone again. "All right, Mme. Levasseur," he said. "We'll try to get your pictures. Can you give us coordinates specifying the area you want photographed? And can you tell us where you'd like us to land, if we can?"

She had the coordinates ready. She read off a string of numbers describing a rectangular area cutting across the mountain range from west to east.

"No good," said Pete. "Too wide. Narrow it by half."

Nathan relayed the message back. The woman didn't seem too worried. She paused for a few moments, then gave us new specifications, cutting the area to be surveyed to a narrow corridor about thirty miles wide.

"I can do that," said Pete, "except that it'll be tapered toward the eastern end—we'll be getting lower all the way."

While Nathan confirmed this I peered closely at the map, trying to see something interesting in the specified area. Pete had turned away now to the control room, but Karen was still with me.

"Nothing but volcanoes," she muttered.

"Mostly dead ones," I observed. But the really curious thing was that the mountains were a hell of a long way east of the fertile land where the ships should have landed. Not only should there be no people there, but there seemed little enough reason for there to be people in the land to the east of them. It was good enough land but it was a long way from site prime. Unless, of course, the ships hadn't put down where they were supposed to.

"People can spread out a lot in a hundred and fifty years," said Conrad, from behind my shoulder.

I nodded. But all I could bring myself to say was, "Maybe."

I turned my attention back to the radio conversation. Helene Levasseur was saying something about possibly being able to show us what she wanted to find out if and when we got the pictures. Then her voice faded out as the bulk of Geb interposed itself between us. Colonies don't have relay satellites to enable conversations with orbiting ships to proceed uninterrupted.

"See to the cameras, Karen," Pete requested.

Karen looked at me, shrugged, and then disappeared into the control room, shutting the door behind her.

"If we can get the pictures," I said to Nathan, "perhaps we won't need her to show us what she's looking for. We can spot it ourselves."

He ignored the statement. Instead, he said, "This is a better welcome than we've had elsewhere. She didn't deny that Geb has problems, she didn't show the least sign of wanting to refuse our help. In fact she's too keen by half to use us. We've dropped into a live situation of some sort . . . she already had a problem and she was quick enough to see how she could fit us into it. I only hope that we aren't helping out in a civil war."

"If there's a rebel army in the mountains," I said sarcastically, "a few aerial photographs of their position isn't going to help much. And who'd want to chase them anyhow?"

But there was a more serious side to the question he'd raised. Geb was the third of the colonies we were scheduled to visit that had been established on a world which already had intelligent indigenes—humanoid creatures that the kingpin of the survey team had named Sets. On Wildeblood humans and aliens hadn't ever come close enough to rub shoulders, though there were some pretty sinister possibilities hanging about in the background. On Attica, though, things had been different. Even with an ocean separating them, humans and aliens—thanks to a little unscheduled intercourse—had been building up for some kind of confrontation. By all accounts the Sets were peaceable vegetarians, and the survey team had been content to observe them from a distance. But a hundred and fifty years of human colonization could change a situation.

Those were the lines Nathan was thinking along too. "The Sets were loosely spread across two continents, right?" he said.

"Sure," I confirmed. "Imhotep—which comes close to touching Akhnaton in the southeast corner—and Akhnaton. But only the eastern half. In the western half, where the colony was supposed to begin operations, they're pretty sparse. But their range is vast—no need to read much into the fact that it includes the Isis mountains."

"No," he agreed. "No need at all." I could tell that he had a hunch, though.

Pete's voice came over the intercom. "Five minutes," he said. "Then the descent begins. It'll be just as usual. No trouble at all."

He shouldn't have said that. It was what some people might call tempting fate.

And fate, like Oscar Wilde, can resist anything but temptation.

At first I thought I'd broken something. But I wasn't yet at the age where my bones had turned brittle. I was severely shaken but still in working order. After all, I'd only fallen off a chair, even if the floor had seemed to come up at me with alarming aggressiveness.

Nathan had been hurled clear across the cabin. He was all right too, but the extent to which he might not have been was obvious. He'd been clutching the hand-mike which patched him through to the main communications apparatus, and through which he'd been talking to Helene Levasseur. The connection had been ripped clean out of the console. It takes quite a jolt to shear through that kind of plastic, let alone the wire core.

I staggered to the door connecting the main cabin to the control room, but it opened before I got there. Karen stepped out, looking as sprightly as ever.

"I was strapped in," she announced proudly.

"Why the hell couldn't you warn us?" I demanded. "We could have taken to our bunks."

"It was a bit of a surprise," she said. "Pete didn't realize we couldn't make it until it was too late to shout. He was busy, anyhow. We overheated. We're going to have to do those repairs all over again."

"You're lucky you don't have to repair us, too," said Nathan, coldly. "Where would we be if Alex and Conrad got smashed up? They're the ones who mend people, remember?"

I changed direction and went for the other door, intending to check on Conrad, Mariel and Linda. With luck, they *would* have been on their bunks. Behind me I heard

Pete begin to talk. He was somewhat more profuse in his apologies than Karen had been. It was the first time he'd had to ditch us, and we'd got around to trusting him. His self-respect was a bit battered.

I looked into the lab on my way past to make sure that nothing had shaken loose, but everything was okay there. Provision had been made in the packing arrangements for the occasional bump, and we were people of fairly neat habits.

Conrad met me in the narrow corridor. He was the oldest member of the crew and the one most at risk, but he'd been lying down. Even without the straps securing him he'd only bounced up and down a couple of times, and wasn't even shaken. Mariel hadn't been so lucky. She'd been dumped on to the floor and had made contact with the outside of her knee. She was white with the pain and it was already beginning to swell. I picked her up and put her back on the bunk, and left Conrad to take care of the injury while I looked for Linda. She, too, had joined the crowd by now, and she was obviously all right. She was tough enough to stand a little jolting.

"What happened?" she asked.

"We ditched," I said. "The shield overheated and we wobbled. We came in a little steeper than we intended and hit the ground too soon. We were bloody lucky to miss the mountain peaks. The computer must have given up the ghost four thousand feet up. Now you know why we have a pilot."

"Any damage?" asked Conrad, flexing Mariel's knee and bringing forth a cry of pain.

"Same sort of repairs we did on Attica," I said. "So Karen says."

"No bones broken," Conrad told Mariel. "But the bruising's bad. You'll have fluid on the joint for a while. Stay in bed."

"Thanks," she muttered.

"I got your lousy photographs," said Karen, her voice

floating out into the corridor because it was overly loud even by her standards. I didn't hear Nathan's reply. I tried to get past Linda to get back into the main cabin, but eventually had to push her in ahead of me.

When I got there Nathan was holding up the dead mike and its wrecked plug for Karen's inspection. She didn't seem too worried. She simply nodded toward the control room. Nathan scrambled through the hatchway to the main communications console, where he quickly re-established contact with Helene Levasseur and began explaining what had happened. Pete said nothing, and took no notice of him though they were mere inches apart. He was engrossed in itemizing the damage to the ship's systems.

"Nothing drastic," Karen assured me. "We can fly home on stand-by. As long as no one wants us to take pictures of the Andes while we head for a landing in the Amazon basin."

I stared with fascination at the displays on the main screen as the computer ran its thorough check of the ship's instrumentation and controls. I could hardly understand any of it, but there was a kind of hypnotic compulsion in the shifting red figures.

"It makes you go blind," commented Karen, though she was staring too. For her, it was okay. She knew what it all meant.

Nathan shut the door of the control room to avoid distraction. Linda had picked up the thin paper map that had been on the table—it was a print-out sheet showing most of the southeast corner of Akhnaton.

"Where are we?" she asked.

Karen considered it for a moment, then stabbed a finger at a spot which looked to me to be well within the mountain range.

"Give or take a thumbnail," she said. "We were supposed to come down *here*." Her finger indicated a spot which must have been several hundred miles farther east and several thousand feet farther down. I looked for the scale indicated at the side of the print-out to check my estimate. It was near enough.

"Where's this town that our lovely siren claims to inhabit?" I asked.

Karen's finger moved a little way south, and then described a rough circle. "Somewhere around here," she said.

"If the only way to get up here is by donkey," I said, "she's going to be a long time getting up here to meet us."

"Those are only the foothills," said Linda, "compared to what we just missed. We must have shaved the tops off the mountains."

"Good job they're volcanic," I joked, weakly. "If they'd had proper peaks instead of craters. . . ."

Nathan stuck his head round the door. "She says she's sorry," he said.

"Did you thank her?" asked Karen.

"She wants to know if we got her pictures. I said we had some, but the unscheduled stop interfered somewhat. We have plenty of time to look them over, though. She says that she can make the first seventy or eighty miles by lorry, but that she's not sure how much farther she can get before she has to start walking—or riding, at any rate. It's going to take several days before she can get to us. It's a long way—up as well as along."

"We know," I told him.

"Before the crash," said Karen, in a thoughtful tone, "I had some print-out . . . not the shots of the mountains . . . the standard spy-eye stuff from a long way up. The computer analysis seemed crazy, but I hadn't time to check it out because of getting ready for the special shots. I'll take a look now."

She moved to the computer console and called up the images that the computer had put together from the high-altitude pictures. By image-intensification and augmentation the computer was supposed to be able to map out cultivated land and such industrial activity as oil refining and iron smelting—in fact, anything causing significant hot-spots where no hot-spots ought to be. She had an image displayed on the screen which showed the whole land surface on Mercator projection, and then cut it down rapidly to show Akhnaton and the greater part of Imhotep, ignoring the two minor land masses.

"It can't be right," she said, immediately.

I could see what she meant. The computer was telling us that by its calculations ninety percent of Akhnaton was under cultivation and most of Imhotep too. The hot spots were widely spaced but were distributed across both continents. Taken literally, that implied that Geb had a population in the hundreds of millions. That didn't make sense. Unless. . . .

"Remember Attica," I said.

On Attica, one of the colonists had discovered a vocation which involved helping the aliens to build an empire and a civilization. In a few short generations he had worked wonders. But he had done nothing on this scale. The colonists of Geb had had longer, but this was balanced out by the fact that the natives of Geb hadn't been nearly as advanced to start with as the primitive Ak'lehrian Empire. In their natural state they had no technology at all—not even fire.

"If that's real," said Linda, "then this is success on a scale we couldn't have dreamed possible."

Nathan came out to take a look. He didn't say anything, but he stared long and hard. Finally, he said: "It's impossible. There must be a malfunction."

"This is integrated from information the cameras took in while we were a long way up," said Karen. "The computers were in perfect order. It may be a bug. There was a lot of cloud cover in the west and across Imhotep. It could be wrong—but it's difficult to see how it could manufacture all those extra hot spots. You'd better check it with your charming friend on the ground."

"Three thousand people given six generations . . ." began Linda, as Nathan disappeared again.

"Forget it," advised Karen. "Rabbits could do it. Not people. If they worked at breeding full time they'd just about make it. But a colony can't just use its women as breeding machines. They're half the labor force too." She pursed her mouth as she noticed the unconscious pun, but no one had the bad taste to comment upon it.

"They would need something like ten children each," admitted Linda. "Every woman, every generation, and starting as young as possible. It doesn't seem very likely."

"I make it more than that," I said, struggling desperately with the mental arithmetic. "More like seventeen or eighteen children each."

"I think this is rather futile," opined Karen. She was probably right.

"If it's true," I said, "it has to be humans plus aliens. And even so it's a miracle."

"The analysis checks out," said Karen, blanking the screen. "If it's a bug it's a consistent bug."

"So get the prints," I said. "All of them—high-altitude stuff, the ones you took over the mountains, the lot. We can see with our own eyes."

"It's an awful lot of paper," said Karen, dubiously.

"We can recycle it," I pointed out, impatiently.

"Yes *sir*," she said. I wasn't about to be impressed by the sarcasm.

Nathan reappeared to tell us that according to Mme. Levasseur the population of the world was considerably less than a million. Asked about the Set population she had confessed ignorance. She had not said anything to indicate that the Sets participated in human civilization, but she had not said anything specifically to the contrary. She appeared to have embarked upon a policy of being evasive.

"Ask her why they have two whole continents under

cultivation to feed a few hundred thousand people," I suggested.

"That's not strictly true," observed Karen. "What the display showed was the distribution of cultivated land rather than the gross amount. It may be that they've just spread themselves out thinly. There weren't a *vast* number of hot spots—they were just much more widely scattered than we expected. Maybe they carved up the continents with the aid of a map and a ruler and gave the original colonists a small nation apiece."

"Some of them must have had a long walk," I commented acidly.

"She says that she'll try to get to us as soon as possible," said Nathan, ignoring the idle banter. "Within a week, she hopes."

"Great," I muttered.

"I'll sign off now," he said. "Give us time to collect ourselves. I'll tell her we have to pick up the pieces."

By this time Conrad had arrived from Mariel's cabin, and I brought him up to date with a few terse and well-chosen sentences.

He seemed less taken aback by the revelation than we had. He simply said: "The aliens."

"If that's so," I said, "they must have come on a hell of a way in a hundred and fifty years. From virtual animality to integration in a fast-developing civilization."

"It must be the aliens," said Linda, suddenly. "The range of the hot spots and the cultivation is practically the same as their range. Wherever there were aliens the humans have migrated. It can hardly be a coincidence."

The computer began to generate paper in vast quantities at Karen's behest, and I stepped over to help her pull it out of the way. The stack of photographs multiplied with awesome speed and efficiency. There were an awful lot of them.

The old question, which had been displaced from my mind by the new mysteries, suddenly returned.

Why on Earth—or on Geb—did Helene Levasseur want aerial photographs of the Isis mountains?

"None of this makes any sense," I said, with a faint note of complaint in my voice. "It's going to drive us all mad if we're going to have to wait a week even to *begin* to find out what's going on."

Karen stood up with the last armful of photographs. She had some difficulty in balancing them on the mound of paper already occupying the table.

"That's the lot," she said. "The answer just *might* be in there. Start looking."

As I stared at the stack my heart sank a little. It looked as if it would take us a week to *look* at them all.

"Oh well," I said. "These things are sent to try us."

"And this time," put in Nathan, "they may well succeed."

❀ 3 ❀

I set the cup of coffee down at Karen's elbow and congratulated her on her devotion to duty. She looked up from the photograph which she had been earnestly studying.

"I'm on shift anyhow," she reminded me. "It's you that's crazy."

"Curiosity kills cats," I observed, "but it only drives men mad."

It was, according to the ship's time we'd been keeping for the last twelve days, the early hours of the morning. Outside, though, the day had already dawned. The day here was a little long, but assuming that the locals still cut it into twenty-four bits they would probably have called it eight o'clock. On the other hand, if they had been sensible enough to forget transition and use metric time, they'd call it by some designation that would be just about meaningless to my poor habit-damned brain.

Everyone else was in bed. One by one they'd realized what a mammoth task was involved in hunting through pictures of hundreds of thousands of square miles of mountain range without knowing what to look for and secure in the knowledge that it probably wasn't there anyhow.

What we *had* found out, from the shots taken higher up, was that the computer had not lied. The population of Geb, be it human or alien or both, really was scattered across two continents, bringing fairly impressive tracts of ground under cultivation in widely separated regions and mining for fuels and ores in locations strung out across half the world. There were only three or four things that looked like towns and they weren't very big. Even allow-ing for the cloud cover it seemed dubious that we'd missed any conglomeration of any real size. The people of Geb didn't seem to be very gregarious. In fact they seemed to be getting about as far away from one another as possible. There had been one major visual clue to the technological status of the colony, and that was an impressive one, though I wasn't sure what interpretation to put on it. They were good road-builders. Their highways were very long and very straight. They had one road which went east-west practically all the way across Akhnaton, skirting the Isis Mountains to the north but otherwise having scant respect for geographic features. From this main artery other roads extended, crossing hundreds of miles—and several extended well over a thousand—to other "towns" or even to large homestead. Each of these minor roads also had its proliferations. You don't build roads like that for horses, and you don't build them overnight either. The colonists obviously had progressed as far as the internal combustion engine, and that in itself was a minor miracle. But they also must have a workforce of *very* considerable size.

"I think we're wasting our time," said Karen. "If Nathan can't prise any more information out of the woman, then we're completely at sea. I reckon that a little plain bargaining is in order."

"We're not here to bargain," I said, patiently—knowing that she knew well enough—"we're here to offer our services. They're entitled to be secretive, or rude, or hostile, or suspicious. We're not supposed to react in kind, even though the temptation at times be great." I said it knowing that I, too, had succumbed to temptation on occasion and retaliated. But this was a new world and the resolutions were still fresh.

"The computer pattern-scan turned up nothing," muttered Karen. "It's pointed out a dozen pretty craters and some nice rock formations, but nothing else. Even if there's something in the mountains as a whole, do you realize what a thin slice of them we've got on these pics? We were pretty low before we ditched. You could draw the area we've got as a thick-leaded line on a standard map."

"I wonder why she chose that line?" I said. "It's only inclined a few degrees to the line of latitude, but it's considerably distant from the line of latitude which passes through the position she gave us as her own. She didn't mind us landing a hundred miles away from her if it would allow us to scan this particular area. When Pete said the first area was too broad she shortened it both sides to hold the same central corridor. Can you sort out the line of pictures which shows the territory dead center of the area—the central five miles or so."

"She didn't know the exact whereabouts of what she wanted to find," Karen pointed out. "She said it might take years of searching on the ground." Even while she was complaining she was checking the serial numbers on a stack of photographs, sorting out the ones I wanted. I took another set and began doing likewise.

"True," I admitted, "but she has *some* reference point somewhere—a place to start at and work out from. And it must be on this central line somewhere."

It took us ten minutes to extract the sequence of shots we wanted, and a further ten to arrange them in the correct order.

"Incidentally," I said, as I began spreading them around the floor in a long curve that spiraled around the table and then began to overlap itself, "as we'll have passed directly overhead of all these points, I guess we're on this line too."

"Sure," she said, extending a foot to tap the last photograph in the sequence and then moving it on a few inches to the non-existent frame which would have been next. "We're about *here*. If you look west out of the ship's cameras you should be able to see this ridge and the peak way back here."

I tiptoed over the layout to the console and got an

image of the outside on the display screen. I rotated the scanner. "There's the ridge," she said. "And the middle one of those three peaks is the one under my big toe."

I looked down at the floor. "And the other two?"

"They're on the parallel sets of pictures."

It gave me a place to start. I began with the bit of empty floor that was our own position and began crawling along the spiral. My gaze went over the ridge—actually quite a gentle bump that was presumably a saddle strung between two mountains and separating two valleys—and then down a long shallow shope. The pictures were mottled with expanses of bare rock, rough grass and occasional areas of shrub. The farther down I went the greater grew the proportion of shrub, but there was very little heavily wooded land. At the bottom of the valley I crossed a stream and admired the lushest vegetation around, and then started climbing again—another long, shallow slope. There was nothing steep enough here to shield the bottom of the bowl from the wind, and I guessed that during the rainy season the storms could get pretty violent, which explained why the hold of the vegetation was a little precarious even though we were below the theoretical altitude of the tree line. I continued up the slope for a couple of frames, and was getting quite exhausted by the energy-sapping toil I could feel in my imagination.

Then I came to a much steeper upslope which reared to a narrow ridge and then plummeted again into a great elliptical bowl—an egg-shaped crater. Here, because of the high walls, there *was* protection from wind, and the inside of the crater had taken full advantage of that fact. Here, as nowhere else, there was a truly rich *flora*—and no doubt *fauna* too. The long axis of the crater was about ten miles in extent—or so I estimated, because it ran slantwise across the track, and the corner of it was chopped off—while the shorter axis was about seven.

"Look at that!" I said.

Karen looked at it, then referred back to the computer scan we had carried out on the pictures.

"The computer sorted that one out," she said, as if that made it immediately uninteresting.

"It's a funny-looking crater," I said. "And it's in a funny place. It's not on top of a mountain—in fact it's on the lower slopes. That long hill continues from the other ridge, up and up and up. And look at these lines at the northern wall. They must be fissures of some kind. These blurry wisps *here* and *there* might be vapor being blown out of them. And what are *these*, half-hidden by the trees?"

Karen got down on her hands and knees to look, but realized immediately how stupid we must have looked. She picked up the two frames containing most of the crater and put them back on the table where we could inspect them in a civilized manner. I checked the serial numbers and started riffling through the piles in search of the missing bit of the crater.

"They look to me," said Karen, "rather like circular tents. But I wouldn't swear to it. No one would. And over here might be the roof of a cabin. But we're at the limits of resolution here and my eye is going crazy trying to make it out."

"If we had an overlapping frame," I said, "we could rig up a stereoscope and get a 3-D image."

She shook her head. "We weren't taking them that quickly," she said. "These are just broken bits of what was actually a much larger image."

"I think you're right about the tents and the cabin," I said, after long perusal and due consideration. "Someone's in the crater. Mme. Levasseur didn't mention that. If she knows about it, then the crater might be the point by which she set our course and selected the area for scanning. If she doesn't know. . . ."

". . . it might be what she's looking for."

I pondered. "What kind of crater do you think that is?" I asked her.

"Volcanic," she answered. "What else?"

"Elliptical in shape? On the lower slopes of a mountain?"

She shrugged. "What both of us know about vulcanology could be written on the back of a postage stamp," she pointed out. Which was true enough.

She picked up another print from the floor and showed it to me. This was the one which included the actual mountain peak—the middle one of the three we could see through the scanner. There was no mistaking that one. It was volcanic all right, though seemingly long extinct. It had a big, deep cone which had solidified a long time ago. This crater too was filled with vegetation now, though it was by no means so rich as that in the egg-shaped crater, being several thousand feet higher up.

"So okay," I said. "Way back when there was a double blast, with fire belching out of the side of the mountain as well as the cone. I guess volcanoes aren't any tidier than the rest of nature."

"It could hardly be the crater itself that Mme. Levasseur is looking for," said Karen, picking up another thread. "It's on the survey team's maps, and it's clearly visible from the slopes of the three peaks we can see. But if the people encamped in it are. . . ."

She stopped then.

"Escaped criminals?" I suggested. "Leaders of the revolution? Escaped slaves?"

We exchanged a slightly significant glance. The last one was hardly likely to be true, but it *did* touch upon a point we'd both considered privately. It takes a big workforce to build thousands of miles of road, the colony had spread out to occupy all the lands that the Sets had formerly possessed, and the Sets were noted in the survey reports as being conspicuously docile. Mme. Levasseur had been very cagey about the population and the aliens—but if you were a colony who had worked wonders by enslaving the indigenes, would you brag about it to the first mission from the supposedly high-minded United Nations of Earth?

"That crater's only about fifty miles away," I said. "I could walk it in a day."

"There isn't a highway," Karen pointed out.

"No, but those slopes are very shallow. And there's no obstruction worthy of the name. With the day here being as long as it is, and this being summer hereabouts, there must be nearly twenty hours daylight in our terms. I could do it."

"Fifty miles is a hell of a long way," she said.

"I'm fit. And I'm also interested. If that's Dr. Livingstone I'd love to play Stanley."

"Sure," she said. "And I'm She-who-must-be-Obeyed."

"You have to stay with the ship anyhow," I pointed out. "More repairs. Anyhow, it's less than fifty. Maybe only forty. Depends how far off the edge of this last print we are. It can't be all that far—I can see that peak clearly enough and that's a good twenty miles farther on."

"You can see a long way in the mountains," she said, "when you're looking at other mountains."

I eyed the clock speculatively. "I can sleep most of the day," I said. "Then put the idea to Nathan late this afternoon. We could make an early start, assuming he wants to come too."

She shrugged. I couldn't tell whether it was because she thought it was a dumb idea or because she wouldn't be able to come along. "Mme. Levasseur isn't going to like it," she said, ominously.

"I'm sure Nathan can put it to her in a way that makes it very difficult for her to forbid it. Besides which, she can't forbid it without giving us a reason, and that would mean giving up her policy of playing the cards so close to her chest."

I paused, then added: "One of these days we'll land on a world where everything is nice and straightforward."

"Hardly," she replied. "Our next stop's the least straightforward place in the universe."

✵ 4 ✵

It was, of course, a good idea in principle. The words "fifty miles" roll off one's tongue so lightly, and the words "less than fifty miles" have a positively enthusiastic tone about them. But our mouths have more ambition than our feet. Words, whatever common parlance may say, speak a great deal more loudly than actions. By the time we'd walked for three hours the distance still to be covered no longer seemed like an easy prospect. It seemed to have stretched to mammoth proportions.

It had been easy enough to talk Nathan into coming along. He was exasperated by the annoyingly secretive Helene Levasseur, who was on her way to "find" us and to "rescue" us, but who was in the meantime taking pains to see that nothing disturbed our blissful ignorance of the way things were on Geb. Nathan had tackled her with the information that there seemed to be people up here in the mountains, camped in an elliptical crater a mere day's walk away. She admitted that she'd known of the man's presence somewhere in the vicinity—she gave his name as Johann Gley and spoke as if there were only one of him—but she advised us to stay away from him, on what seemed to be the rather slender excuse that he was not known for his sociability.

When Nathan made it clear that we intended to make contact she was obviously peeved but merely repeated that it wasn't a good idea. She came forth with no hints whatsoever about what Gley might be doing up here. When asked point blank she said she didn't know, and added the acid comment: "He owns the mountains." She didn't seem delighted by the fact. She assured us that she was on her way up into the hills with a party of Sets and would reach us in four or five days, provided that there were no accidents *en route*. Whether her estimate was reasonable we had no way of knowing. Nathan asked if the other individuals who appear to be in the crater with Gley were also Sets, and she replied that it was probably a reasonable inference. That wasn't telling us anything we couldn't have worked out for ourselves—and, indeed, was bordering on insult.

Nathan tried to make light of the issue. "She doesn't trust us," he said. "And why should she. She thinks we've come to make some kind of report on what's happened on this world. And she's right. She probably thinks that the UN might disapprove strongly of certain things that might have happened—and might be happening—here. And she's probably right. She's worried about what, if anything, we or the people we report to might do about it. There she probably has nothing to worry about, in that there's very little we *can* do. But she doesn't know that and she isn't going to take *our* word for it. She wants a good, long, close look at us before she starts to tell us what we want to know."

But it is no real consolation to know that the mistrust of others is to a large extent justified. It still left us in the frustrating position of speculating much and knowing little. And so we elected to take action. Nathan fell in with my plan, and we set out shortly after dawn on the next day, with a long, long walk ahead of us. It took, as I said, about three hours for much of our enthusiasm to drain away through tired feet—but by then we were committed.

We rested on a patch of bare ground that was cold beneath our backsides. Although it was summer the air was crisp, and when the wind blew it cut into our faces. But it was by no means unpleasant once we grew used to it, and the continuous action of our muscles kept us warm enough internally. There was no snow here, although the distant peaks we could see all had white patches on the high slopes. There was a low murmurous sound made by insects meandering through patches of flowering plants that interrupted the coarse grasses. Occasionally we could hear birds calling, though none came very close except when we skirted great carpets of prostrate thorn-creepers which had purple berries on which the smaller birds fed.

"It's downhill for a long way now," I said.

"Then it's uphill for a long way," said Nathan, choosing to look on the dark side. "With maybe a few bumps and ditches thrown in for variety."

"It's easy country," I reminded him. "And if we have to camp out for the night we can." We had only light packs, but we'd prudently packed sleeping bags. We had a small radio to keep in touch with the *Daedalus,* but· it wasn't very powerful. Our number one mobile communications apparatus had been lost along with a lot of other equipment on Attica.

"While you were asleep," he said, changing the subject, "I asked Mariel what she made of Helene Levasseur's voice. There was something in her tone I thought odd. I didn't expect much—Mariel's talent for thought-reading depends much more on sight than on sound—but Mariel thought it was odd too. There's some anxiety in her voice that was there from the very first moment. Quite apart from the shock of our arrival. It was as though when we turned up it was just an extra problem on the stack—an additional inconvenience. Asking us to get those pictures was a spur-of-the-moment thing, and since we had to ditch I think she's been half regretting it. On the one hand she wants the pictures, but on the other she's not sure she wants *us* to have them. I think Gley's up here looking for something, and she wants to find it too. Something important."

"El Dorado?"

"Wrong scale of values."

"The Fountain of Youth, then."

Nathan shook his head. "It's a little more pressing than that."

"The survey team did an aerial scan of the whole continent for mapping purposes," I said. "But what she wants obviously didn't show up there."

"They took their shots from too high up. On their survey this crater would have shown up no bigger than my little fingernail, even at the limits of resolution. Okay for mapping, but useless for anything else."

"Like what?"

"You know as well as I do what kind of things show up well from the air. Evidence of cultural interference. Archaeological sites and records of natural disasters. Wherever the vegetation changes its color or its pattern because the soil has been turned over or otherwise altered."

"There are plenty of natural disasters hereabouts," I commented. "But the eruption record of the volcanoes isn't likely to worry them much. Vegetation shadows of archaeological sites . . . but the aliens never built so much as a mud hut, so far as we know."

"So far as we know," he echoed.

"But now they're enslaved, and they live in little round tents. In the wild, they were pre-cultural. No language beyond a range of animal grunts. No permanent tools. No fire. But they've adapted now, very quickly and very well."

"If you'd built a culture based on the services of adaptable, docile aliens, and had spread yourself very thin across two continents, and you were outnumbered by several hundred to one by your slave-race . . . mightn't you begin to wonder? Mightn't a little anxiety creep in, slowly and insidiously?"

"Vegetation shadows," I repeated, letting my imagination roam. "I didn't see anything . . . and why here, of all places? This is the *last* place on the continent to look for traces of a vanished civilization."

He shrugged. "So maybe it's the Fountain of Youth," he said.

We set off again, setting a steady, sensible pace. As we descended into the valley toward the stream that ran across the shallow bowl the going got a little tougher because of the more abundant vegetation, especially the thorny creepers. But there were always expanses of bare rock and thin grass, and it was easy enough to find a route that didn't take us far off the straight course we'd plotted out for ourselves. Farther down we even spotted a small herd of wild donkeys—perhaps twenty or twenty-five strong—grazing on the slope. They moved off while we were still a couple of hundred meters distant, and I had a brief pang of regret regarding my lost binoculars, but it soon passed. They were, of course, a native life form, but they could actually have passed for Earthly donkeys in a dim light. They were ready-made pack animals, though they walked a little slowly to be ideal as riding animals except where the terrain was really rough.

Once a bird of prey swooped across the scrub a short distance ahead of us, in pursuit of some small creature, but it must have reached its bolt-hole. The bird soared up into the sky again, empty-clawed. Half an hour later I saw it swoop again, but this time another bird went for the same target and they ended up having a go at one another instead, cawing madly. A couple of dark feathers fluttered to the ground before they went their separate ways. It looked like a lean day for them so far—but they had lots of time. A hawk has only to be patient, because it usually wins in the end. The creatures on the ground have to go about their own business, taking their daily risks and hoping at best to survive. But nothing bothers the hawk up in the sky.

There were trees here, but they clustered in patches of ten or a dozen, and for the most part they were weedy specimens, with tall thin trunks extending eight or ten feet up and then spreading out clusters of branches like the kind of imitation bouquets that conjurors produce from their wands. The soil up here grew deep in grooves where wind and weather had eroded the lava which had spilled out of the ground long, long ago, but there was always more wind and more weather, and the bedrock was too close to the surface. The vegetation pattern here must change with the decades. Only permanent soil holds shadows. If that was really what Mme. Levasseur hoped to see she'd have to look at valleys deeper and steeper than this great saucer we were crossing now.

We came to a region where the thorn sprays formed great carpets, looking for all the world like brownish lakes with waves and whirlpools. Most of the foliage hereabouts was brown or gray-green, and all in darker shades.

We had to stop again soon. We were having trouble with the air, which was thinner than we were accustomed to. I had prescribed carbon pills before we set off, and had packed a couple of the oxygen-bottles that we could use if need be in association with sterile suits should their filters be faced with an impossible job, but we had to use the oxygen sparingly, and it really offered only temporary relief. The carbon pills had little enough effect—I'd never really believed in them on Earth, on the occasions when I'd had to do high-altitude work. If anything were to stop us getting to the crater in one day it was surely going to be the atmospheric pressure.

We tramped on across a wasteland of grass-knotted gravel that lasted for three or four miles, and finally got to the bottom of the saucer, where the thickness of the vegetation finally got to the point where it might impede us. But there was little enough of the thorny stuff here— much of the plant life consisted of brittle-stemmed things like ferns and small flowering plants. We found that the only significant nuisance was caused by tiny insects which settled on our faces and the backs of our hands—attracted perhaps by the moisture or the salt in our sweat. They didn't bite, but one or two of the species apparently went through life secreting or excreting some irritant substance that made us itch.

We found numerous small pools where the water of melted snows or spring rains had collected—some of them quite deep and obviously permanent. They tended to be long and narrow, often curved into thin crescents. The water was murky and rather foul in the small pools, and even the larger ones had a scum of vegetable debris and skimming creatures that might have been larvae of one kind and another. I saw water snails and rafts of eggs and shrimp-like invertebrates. We filtered some water and boiled it to replenish our own supply late in the morning, though it wasn't necessary. It just gave us something to do while we were taking it easy. I calculated how far we'd come and found we were only a few minutes behind schedule.

"They're always the same," said Nathan, who was watching a small flock of birds in the branches of a tree growing by the bank of the pool. "On every world we go to. The plants are different, to some extent, but not the birds. Even large animals are sometimes quite bizarre, but the birds are always the same. It almost asks you to believe that there's a pattern in it all somewhere. When you come down to it, the differences in the intelligent forms are more striking than the similarities . . . especially with the species like the salamen. But you can always find sparrows made in the image of sparrows on Earth. Maybe God's a sparrow."

"Whenever different cultures invent certain things they do it the same way," I pointed out. "Whether it's made by human or alien a wheel is always round. A bow and arrow is always a bow and arrow—even quite complicated things like saddles are made to fit an animal's back one way and a human arse the other. An organism is a kind of technology too. It's an egg's way of making another egg. All eggs look pretty much the same—they're either round or egg shaped. The ways they have of reproducing themselves are pretty much akin, too. An organism is a device; an invention. There are certain forms which are up to the job, and some that are capable of a certain amount of variability on a basic theme. Birds are one of the possibilities where there's relatively little variation possible, and where virtually every possibility tends to be worked out in any one life system. Flying's a good trick. It usually makes for evolutionary security, so what variation there is tends to come out. See?"

"I think so," he replied.

"In the whole of evolutionary history here and on all the Earth-type worlds we've tried to colonize eggs have made exactly two vital inventions," I went on. "The eggshell and the womb. All else is variation on a very few anatomical themes. You could count the internal skeleton as well, I guess, but on some worlds that are pretty far removed from the Earth model but still hospitable enough for us to investigate animal life has got along without that particular invention. It still developed shelled eggs and wombs though. So there is a pattern—a stage-by-stage developmental process—just as there's a pattern of sorts in technological progress. A truly alien world that is nevertheless habitable for man is alien in just one or two respects. Either it missed out on inventing wombs or it missed out on inventing eggshells, or maybe both. We haven't yet found a world that shows us the *other* possibility."

"Which is?"

"Making the third vital invention, of course. We don't know what it is because our life-system hasn't . . . yet."

"I see," he said, again. But perhaps he didn't, because he retreated to his original point. "So birds will always look like birds. And intelligent creatures will be humanoid at least to the extent of being bipedal."

"Not necessarily," I said. "To be intelligent you need a big brain. There's more than one way to arrange that particular mechanical marvel. Upright stance is one, which also frees the forelimbs of a quadruped to grow hands. But another way is to live in the sea, where weight isn't so desperately important. The amphibians of Wildeblood had it both ways. A marine mammal like a dolphin may not have hands, but he can be pretty bright and can develop a language. Even a marine reptile, or perhaps even a fish, *might* do as well, if the chances fell right. Even that might be ultra-conservative, particularly with reference to those worlds where there are no vertebrates. There's no mechanical reason that bans invertebrate nervous systems from growing complex organs and networks. The squid and the octopus are the cleverest Earthly invertebrates, but I don't find it inconceivable that on some world with lots of warm ocean there might be intelligent invertebrates on just about any model. Submarine life is more versatile than life on land—even on Earth quite unremarkable and utterly unintelligent marine invertebrates have a degree of technological control over their environment that puts proto-human apes to shame Barnacles and coral-polyps, tube-building worms and such like things show off the potential.

"Sometimes I wonder whether on a galaxy-wide scale that might be where the *real* potential lies, and that every thing we are and do might be just a useless side-branch in the *really* basic evolutionary schema. On Earth, life was tempted out of the sea . . . and maybe life on Earth won't get back to the evolutionary mainstream until we bizarre land-life experiments abort ourselves with nuclear weapons and a kind of intelligence that may well be self-destructive. Life on Earth—and on all the Earth-type worlds—may hardly have started yet. The oxygen atmosphere might be just a phase that worlds pass through on their way to a maturity we can't imagine. We may be just part of a brief exploratory digression that can only come to nothing in the end.

"The oceans were there before the particular atmosphere we call natural, and the oceans may still be there when that atmosphere is changed into something else by the ongoing chemical processes of life. When we go out into local space searching out worlds like ours we may be seeking out only those in a particular stage of immaturity, or maybe worlds that have become stuck in a kind of dead end. Maybe the places where the *real* pattern is—the places where the *real* story of life in the universe is being acted out—are places very different from this one. Our delusions may be just a cosmic joke. Maybe true alienness does exist at a level of intelligence we can't comprehend . . . and we can never come to terms with it; never reach it; never coexist with it; never be a part of it."

"Bad attack of philosophy you have there," said Nathan, dismissively.

I was uncomfortably aware of the fact that I was blushing.

"Don't worry," I said. "It isn't catching. Though it was you that started it."

"Even if it were all true," he said—oddly enough, I think he was trying to reassure me as though I'd just confessed some terrible existential doubt—"*il faut cultiver notre jardin*. Quite candidly."

"I never wanted to suggest anything else," I told him. "This is where *we* belong. This and all the worlds like it. This is our universe and all the others don't matter a damn until we bump into some chlorine-breathing octopodes driving their starship through the vasty deep . . . and even then we can content ourselves with saying "hello" and passing on our separate ways. The plan of life in the universe and its ultimate destiny is nothing whatsoever to do with *us*. There isn't any implication for human existence in anything I've said. We're entitled to be anthropocentric, and we'd be fools to be anything else. But it doesn't do any harm to speculate. Sometimes . . . only sometimes . . . I think it might even do us good. To see ourselves as others might see us, as we really might *be* in terms of the cosmos itself and its own history. As God might see us, if you like."

"But He isn't a bird. He's a giant squid."

"I don't know. Nobody can. I can't imagine God . . . but I see no reason why an anthropomorphic God should be any more likely than a crinoid or holothuridean God in terms of what actually might be the pattern and the plan of universal life."

"You take it too seriously," he told me.

"No doubt," I replied. "No doubt."

❀ 5 ❀

Inevitably, we couldn't make it. Three things stopped us. First, there was too much up and down. Fifty miles on a map looks flat, but it takes a bird of prey to fly it that way. Not being hawks, Nathan and I found the real distance too far. Secondly, we weren't wholly fit. It had been quite some time since I'd done any serious hiking—even my adventures on Attica had been widely separated by long periods at sea where there was nowhere to walk at all. Thirdly, of course, there was the thin air which wasn't rich enough for our unacclimatized lungs to suck out all the oxygen our bodies needed. The occasional sniff at an oxy-bottle just wasn't enough to compensate. After our noon break we fell steadily further behind the block. The last straw came when we realized that our calculations about the length of the day were over-optimistic because we had neglected the minor point that there was a mountain due west of us, which cut out the sun's light fifty minutes before we had reckoned on it getting dark.

We had brought one fairly large lamp as a standard precaution, and there was also a small flashlight. Between them they cast enough light for us to see our way by, and the dying shades of dusk showed us the ramparts of the crater's rim tantalizingly close, but we paused to rest and think it over.

"It's no more than five miles," I said, as I lay on my back and watched the stars come out in the clear sky above. There were a great many stars, with the milky way itself drawing a ribbon of faint light across the northern horizon. It would have been a nice place to build an observatory.

"Once inside the crater it's bound to be more difficult," he said. "The vegetation there is different from anything we've met so far."

"It won't be impenetrable," I told him. "We're too high up for dense jungle. There may be a lot more trees but the great majority will be just as weedy as the ones we've seen. And it's getting cold. It'll be a miserable night if we spend it out here on the exposed slope. If we get to Gley he's likely to have a fire and four wooden walls to contain the heat. Even if he's the most anti-social man on Geb he'll hardly turn us away from his door. If he tries we can always mention aerial photographs to see if his mouth waters."

The prospect of spending the night in the open didn't endear itself to Nathan. The air had grown noticeably colder since the sun's light was cut off, and there was still a breeze that chilled the flesh in a rather unpleasant manner.

I called the ship and told them what had happened, and that we were going on in the hope that the going wouldn't get too tough. It was Karen's shift again and she was manning the radio. She didn't say "I told you so," but she knew I'd remember that she *had* told me so. There was a slightly false note in her sympathy, revealing that deep down she really did have a malicious streak.

When I'd packed the set away again I brushed my beard lightly with my fingertips, and was surprised to find tiny ice crystals making the hairs brittle.

"I'm developing a frost," I told Nathan.

He didn't have any such problem. He was clean-shaven. As a special favor he let me carry the lantern. It qualified as a favor because it produced a certain amount of heat as well as light, and could be modified if need be to turn out heat *instead* of light. As things were, though, I figured we needed the light more, and adjusted it accordingly.

We were climbing quite steeply now, but the slopes

were almost bare of grass and thorn. The rock was solid
but rough—the surface was pitted and cracked in what
seemed to me to be a rather peculiar manner. The climb
was particularly exhausting after a long, hard day, but the
angle was never more than thirty-five or forty degrees and
footholds were plentiful because of the pits and crevices.
By the time we got to the top I was panting very hard,
and had to replenish myself with oxygen from the supply
which was by now getting very low.

We rested again before tackling the downslope, which
was something of a luxury for the first couple of hundred
yards, before the vegetation got thick. As we descended
the bare rock Nathan drew my attention to the little
cracks that ran all over the surface like crocodiling on an
old oil painting.

"I've never seen anything like it," I told him. "But I
haven't spent much time in this kind of country. Might be
something to do with the lava contracting as it cooled.
You know how mud cracks when stream beds dry up in a
drought."

The analogy was false, but I was only trying to say
something that would sound semi-sensible. He didn't com-
plain.

We moved into the richer vegetation, unable to appreciate its wonders because of the absence of daylight. It
wasn't very difficult to begin with, and as it got denser we
picked up what appeared to be an animal trail which led
toward the center of the crater almost as straight as a die.

I thought that was very fortunate. But I was assuming
at the time that our chapter of accidents was over and
that fate had sated itself on temptation.

Dangerous assumptions, those.

And in this case, quite wrong.

Nathan was leading the way now, and I had passed the
lantern on to him. He was holding it high because his
main difficulty was protruding tree branches that stuck
out into the trail. Animals not being as tall as men they

can get by with trails that are effectively tunnels—they have no objection to tree branches. I had the small flashlight, which I was directing up, down and off to the side—wherever the whim took me. I was foolishly inspecting animal droppings, contemplating small fluttering moths and trying to locate a slightly musty odor with something similar in my memory. I should have been concentrating on things that concerned us more directly.

We had gone perhaps three-quarters of a mile along the trail when Nathan simply disappeared from view. The lamp went tumbling with him, its light abruptly cut off from my eyes by the edge of a deep pit.

His mighty cry of annoyance turned sharply into a cry of pain.

I stopped, got down on my hands and knees, and inched forward, testing the ground in front of me with my knuckles. I got to the edge, and I didn't have to shine the beam of the flashlight down into the pit because Nathan and the lantern were lying side by side. The lamp threw up a rather alarming forest of shadows because the bed of the pit contained four upright stakes, each one a meter long and the thickness of my arm, and each sharpened to a point. What Nathan had fallen into was no crevice but a trap.

It suddenly struck me that a very logical place to put a pitfall trap is across an animal trail. The thought that struck me next was that people didn't build pitfall traps like that one unless they wanted to catch something big and nasty.

Mercifully, Nathan had not fallen forwards, but more or less straight down, thus avoiding the spikes calculated to impale him. He had twisted while he fell, trying to reach back and grab the lip of the pit. In so doing he had fallen awkwardly, and one of his legs was twisted now into a position I didn't like at all. His shirt was ripped and his forehead was bleeding, but neither of those injuries was more than a scratch. It was his leg that mattered.

He looked up at me, his face chalk-white and his mouth drawn open in a rictus of pain. I could tell that the prospect of reaching down so that he could grab my arm and pull himself out was simply not on.

I waited for him to control his facial muscles so that he could speak. The only thing I could think of to say was, "Are you all right?" and that would have been too stupid. So I simply waited.

"My leg's broken," he said, when he could get the words out.

"Upper or lower?" I asked.

"Below the knee. Trapped as I fell. Think the shin-bone's gone." He had to stop to gasp, and could say no more for the moment.

I took the pack from my back and moved along the rim of the trap to let it down beyond the prostrate lamp.

"I'm coming down," I said. "I think I can slide into the gap without landing on top of you."

I saw the muscles in his neck tense when he bowed his head and hunched up. I let myself down until I was hanging vertically, with only my hands clutching the rim of the trap. When I let go I had only a couple of feet farther to fall. I didn't think I'd have any real difficulty climbing out again. The walls of the pit were firm enough with clay to be solid, but soft enough for me to scrape out footholds with the toe of my boot. But getting Nathan out was going to be a problem of an entirely different order.

There wasn't much room, but I managed to turn him over and exposed the damaged leg. It was bleeding, but only venous blood. There was no need for a tourniquet. His own diagnosis has been accurate enough—the tibia was fractured. It seemed like a clean break, and the fibula was still in one piece.

I pulled the radio out of my pack and signaled the ship. It was Karen who answered.

"We're in trouble," I said. "Nathan's broken his leg in

a pitfall trap. I can't get him out without help, let alone carry him."

"Where are you?"

"In the crater. We were following an animal trail. Apparently it's used by something other than wild donkeys—something Gley wanted to discourage. At least, I think so. Could be it was meant for human visitors, I guess. Helene Levasseur said he was antisocial."

"What do you want us to do?"

"Nothing now. No point in a rescue mission rushing out by dead of night and getting someone else hurt in a fall. If it has to be a rescue party I'll call again after dawn."

"If you do that," she pointed out, "they'll have exactly the same trouble you did. Darkness will catch up with them before they reach you."

I muttered silent curses. On balance, it would probably be better if a rescue party could set off before dawn and do an hour before daybreak over relatively easier country than start out later and get caught as we had. The only alternative was to do the hike in two stages.

"It might not be necessary at all," I said. "Hang on for a couple of hours. There's help much nearer if I can reach it."

"You're going to leave Nathan in the pit?"

"I don't see any alternative. We have a flashgun, and I guess I could let it off a couple of times in the hope of attracting attention, but I don't know how far away the camp is, and the trees will muffle the sound. I'll give him a shot of pain-killer and something to keep him awake. That way if anything nasty turns up he can at least try to frighten it away. He'll be okay. I'll leave the radio with him."

"In case you don't come back?"

"Don't be so bloody cheerful."

I cut the connection and looked around uneasily at the dimensions of the trap. Determined to find a bright side to look on I told myself how lucky we'd been to fall into the trap instead of meeting up with the creature it was intended for.

I gave Nathan a shot of pain-killer, but I dressed the wound before giving him something to wake him up. There wasn't a lot I could do except ease the bone back into place and bind it up. I turned the lamp down a little to give out more heat, and then tried to get Nathan into his sleeping bag. There just wasn't the room to maneuver, and in the end I gave up and settled for wrapping it around him as best I could. I used my own to wrap up his legs.

I pressed the flashgun into his hands.

"You fit?" I asked.

"I'll manage," he assured me. There was no longer any agonized strain in his voice, and it sounded almost ghostly in its flatness.

Climbing out was easier than I'd expected. I only had to brace myself between the wall of the pit and one of the upright stakes to shove myself high enough to get my arms over the edge. Then it was easy to scramble out. I came up on the side opposite to the one where I'd gone in, carrying nothing but the small flashlight, which I'd stuck in my belt.

The trail went on toward the center of the crater. I scraped a little of the clay off my clothing and went on, keeping a very careful eye on the ground in front of me.

I had been moving for about half an hour when the trail emerged from the trees and was lost. The soil gave way to a series of rounded boulders and a chain of pools. There were leafy plants like lily-pads extending across the surface of the nearest one in long, parallel streamers, with big cup-shaped blue flowers. The boulders didn't form a perfect path through the pools, but there were gaps of about a foot here and there. They could still be used as stepping stones, and I crossed without difficulty. There were trees again on the other side, but more widely spaced, with conical bushes about four feet high standing between them, and open spaces where flowering plants grew in some profusion. I shone the flashlight around, looking for a path of some kind, and soon located one. At first I thought it was another animal trail—or an extension of the same one, but it wasn't. The first trail had been leading to the water hole. So did this one, but it was coming from the opposite direction and it had been worn by humanoid feet encased in shoes or moccasins. The soft soil clearly showed the impressions.

I began to follow the path. Force of habit kept the patch of light cast by the flashlight on the ground in advance of my feet, though it hardly made sense that Gley would lay pitfalls across his own highway. It was because of this that the first time I saw a Set I started with the feet and worked my way up to the curious snout.

The feet were shod in what looked like donkey hide, though the soles were made of wood. The legs could have been human except that they were hairless and colored a strange shade of gray-brown. It was wearing a loincloth and a kind of waistcoat that seemed to be more for decoration than protection against the cold. It was looking at me from two big brown round-pupilled eyes that were set level in its head for binocular vision. It was looking along the ridge of a colossal nose which flared to contain a mouth and a collection of grinding teeth that reminded me of a camel or a llama, though its head, like the rest of its body, seemed quite devoid of hair.

When I lifted the light to shine in its eyes it blinked, and I could see the pupil contract reflexively.

It just stood there, blocking the path, mute.

I felt like a fool. I had been here before and I had *never* carried it off with anything remotely resembling panache. As it was late and I was tired I figured I could be forgiven for not thinking of anything that really befitted the occasion.

"Do you understand English?" I asked.

Maybe he nodded and I just didn't notice.

"If I were to say? 'Take me to your . . .' Oh, forget it. Where's Gley?"

As I spoke I must have stepped forward a little, maybe raising my arm in some kind of reflexive gesture. The Set moved back a step, warily, then turned abruptly on its heel and ran.

I was just wondering what I'd said when some kind of clanging started up ahead. It sounded for all the world like some kind of alarm.

I sighed, and walked on. I half expected to be jumped and hurled to the ground by a dozen Sets, but nothing happened. I came into a clearing about thirty meters from the cabin, and saw the sentry still thumping away with a wooden hammer on a kind of gong hanging from the eaves.

I was halfway across the clearing when the door burst open, and a man I assumed to be Johann Gley appeared, half-dressed and looking very aggressive. In his arms he carried a big double-barreled shotgun that looked as if it would cut me in half if he was a little nervous on the trigger.

Without thinking, I put my hands up. That's what comes of spending your formative years watching too much HV. But when he saw I was human he relaxed a little, letting the gun fall to the level of his waist and pointing the barrels down at the ground well in front of my feet. I put my hands down and walked on.

He was a tall man—a couple of inches taller than I—and his features could only be described as ugly. His forehead was big and square, his nose somewhat squashed. He had prominent cheekbones and a wide chin. He looked very tough—the sort of character whose face would do terrible things to your knuckles if you punched it.

"Who the hell are you?" he demanded, gracelessly.

"My name's Alexis Alexander," I told him. "I'm sorry

I frightened the Set. There was really no need for the alarm."

I glanced around as I said this, wondering where the Set had got to. There was no sign of him—or any others of his species. I couldn't see the tents from here—there were no lights anywhere in the encampment except for some kind of lamp burning in the cabin.

"Shine that light on yourself," said Gley, without bothering to introduce himself.

I complied, letting him look first at my face and then at the rest of me. I knew that the clothes would give him cause to think.

"What are you doing here?" he demanded.

"We were coming to see you. There were two of us, but nightfall caught us just short of the crater wall. We tried to come through the trees along an animal trail—my companion fell into a trap. He has a broken leg."

I turned the light back on Gley in order to measure his reaction. But he still looked puzzled and suspicious. He didn't sympathize—but then, he didn't burst out laughing, either.

"Who sent you?" he growled.

"The United Nations," I told him.

"*Who?*"

"Of Earth," I added, remembering that the fame of the organization wasn't such that every last fifth-generation colonist would instantly recognize it. He didn't say anything, so I couldn't help going on: "It's a little world about eighty-six light years away across the galactic arm."

"From Earth," he echoed. His tone had changed somewhat, as though his mind had changed gear, but I couldn't read anything into the change. Had Mariel been here she could probably have read the thoughts through the shifting involuntary twitches in his face, but hers was a talent and not a skill. I'd never been able to pick up even the first principles.

"We ditched in the mountains," I said. "We didn't intend to land here, but this is our final port of call before returning to Earth. The systems aren't what they used to be. We came in a little too steeply—or maybe a little too shallow—and overheated. The computer gave up in disgust and our pilot improvised."

"Where's your ship?" he asked.

"About fifty miles east."

"Fifty miles! How did you know where to find me?"

"We took some pictures from the air on the way down. Your camp was visible."

I half expected another change of gear as the thought of aerial photographs splashed into his mind, but I was disappointed. It obviously didn't mean to him what it meant to Helene Levasseur—unless he was a slow thinker temporarily lacking in inspiration.

"What do you want?" he asked, again.

"Help," I said. "Some ropes. Something to make a stretcher. Maybe a couple of the aliens could help us. I'm sorry about the accident and for dragging you out of bed, but it is your trap that Nathan fell into."

"You'd better come in," he said.

I came forward again. By the time I got to the steps up to the cabin floor he was inside. I switched off the flashlight and followed him in. There were at least two rooms. He brought his own lamp out of what was presumably his bedroom into the main room. The furniture was a little bit fundamental but the place looked thoroughly lived in. There was a single chair and a big table covered with the debris of at least two meals. There were shelves in considerable quantity covered with boxes containing foodstuffs, jars, tools of various kinds and numerous lumps of rock that had—so far as I could tell—neither purpose nor aesthetic appeal. There was a stone chimney-breast and a large opening decked with various iron grids and gratings, with cooking pots of several different sizes—mostly dirty—standing around the hearth in careless disarray.

There was a fire burning in the grate but it was almost out.

Gley dumped the lamp on the table and then began rooting around in a pile of debris in one corner. There was a lot of rope there but it took him some time to disentangle one length from the others. Then he produced a dirty, ragged blanket and a slightly-rusted machete.

"Have to cut a couple of poles," he muttered. "I'll go rouse a couple of the Sets."

He thrust what he had gathered so far into my arms, and went out. He had been gone only a couple of seconds before he reappeared, grabbed the lamp from the table, and set off again.

Left in darkness, I switched on the flashlight. There didn't seem to be much point in hanging about inside so I went back out on to the verandah and closed the door behind me, shivering in the chilly air.

Gley reappeared after an interval of five minutes, leading two Sets. Whether the one who'd raised the alarm was one of them I couldn't tell.

"This is Ham and this is Shem," said Gley, stabbing a thumb first at one, then at the other, though they looked to me to be identical. "They understand simple English and they'll do what you tell 'em as long as you don't confuse 'em. But you have to make the instructions proper if you're telling 'em to do something new. Better let me handle it an' just keep quiet."

He took the machete from my hand and gave it to the Set he'd called Ham, but didn't start issuing orders about cutting poles.

"Don't they talk?" I asked.

"No," he said, and left it at that. He took the rope from me and gave it to Shem. He left the blanket in my charge. He started out across the clearing.

"Shouldn't you have given them names more in keeping with Egyptological tradition?" I asked, innocently, as I fell into step behind him.

"One lot of names is as good as another," he said. "When you have seventy or eighty Sets you give 'em all the names you can think of . . . and even then you can't remember 'em. Even when you can tell 'em all apart you can't remember which is which. *They* can't tell you. But we get by. They're easy to work with."

"They're . . . slaves?" It wasn't a very diplomatic way to put what might be a delicate question, but it slipped out that way.

He half turned to look back at me.

"Are they?" he said.

"What else?" I asked, thinking I might as well press on.

"They're just Sets," he said. "That's all."

His voice was coarse, and his answers were mounting a shield of of stubborn evasion, but I got the impression that it was at least in part an act. He was fully conscious of what he was doing.

"Why did you come here?" he asked when I didn't venture any other comment on the subject of Sets and slavery.

"We're making contact with a number of colonies," I said. "The space program's been through a lean spell, but the UN managed to get one ship operative to bring some kind of assistance to the colonies. We have a laboratory on board with equipment used in genetic engineering. Most of the colonies are having problems with adapting to alien environments—after a honeymoon period of a couple of generations local life systems start reacting against the invasion. We try to nullify or minimize the effects of their reaction."

"You mean that some of the colonies never made it," he said.

"Some were in grave difficulties. The situation varied a lot from world to world. Not everyone has Sets to share the burden."

Now it was his turn to be silent for a pause while he thought over what I had told him.

"What are *you* doing up here?" I asked. "It's a pretty desolate spot."

"That's my business," he replied. "I like it here."

"And dangerous too," I added, "to judge by the size of that pitfall."

"It's dangerous," he confirmed. "I've lost Sets and donkeys. I haven't even seen whatever it is that kills them, but it does a thorough job of stripping the bones. Carries off limbs sometimes. I had to dig the pit. There's only one of me . . . the Sets don't fight back. They're vegetarian, completely non-aggressive. Won't even defend themselves. All they do is run away . . . and sometimes they get caught."

"But you haven't caught it so far?"

"No," he admitted. "All I've caught is you."

He glanced back over his shoulder again, but there wasn't the ghost of a smile across his flat mouth. I still got the impression, though, that the outside was something of a mask. Inside, he was thinking hard.

"Maybe it's not so bad," I said. "Maybe we can help you find whatever it is you're looking for."

This time he stopped, and I thought I'd startled him until I realized that we were back at the water hole and he was preparing to negotiate the stepping-stones. But he looked sideways at me as I came up abreast of him, and he said: "Maybe you can."

❊ 6 ❊

I got through to Karen again and called off the rescue party while we were making our way back to Gley's cabin. The Sets carried Nathan on an improvised stretcher. He remained awake and alert during the walk, but he didn't have a lot to say either to me or to Gley. As soon as we got back I gave him a new shot—this time to put him to sleep.

Gley nobly gave up his own bed to Nathan, though it was a dubious privilege. He laid out a couple of blankets alongside the bed for me and then wandered off into the night, presumably to share the poor lodging of the Sets. I was prepared to bet that he'd be a damn sight more comfortable than I was on the wooden floor. My legs were aching after the day's exertions and the floor didn't do much to help. But exhaustion is a strong sedative, and I wasn't in need of any shots myself.

I had lousy dreams, though.

When I got up next morning and staggered into the other room the sun was well up in the sky but there was no sign that Gley had been back. The state of disarray looked even worse by daylight than it had the night before. I looked around for something to drink but gave up in despair. There was plenty of stuff around that looked as if it had once been food and might be again if only it received the services of a cunning chef, but nothing looked appetizing. I went back to my pack and took a drink from my own water bottle. I looked at my watch, but I'd omitted to readjust it to local time and it was still ticking off a twenty-four-hour standard day that had been out of phase even to begin with. It told me how many hours I'd been away from the ship but not what time it was likely to be in Gley's terms.

Nathan was still sleeping peacefully, and I didn't disturb him. Instead I went outside on to the verandah. I could see the Sets' encampment away to the right, behind a thin strand of trees. The rounded tents were tepees which looked neatly and competently built. Apparently the Sets learned manual skills easily. I wondered briefly why, if such skills were there waiting to be tapped, they'd developed no technology of their own. It seemed like something of a paradox. But I postponed serious thinking for later.

All was quiet. Not even a Set was stirring, as far as I could tell. I stood there for a few moments, tasting the air. There was a complex mixture of scents drifting upon the slightest of breezes. I looked across at Gley's path to the waterhole, and was surprised to see so many flowers on and around the conical bushes. Mostly they were blue and purple, but there were reds and yellows too in little pockets here and there. The insects were up and about already, and so were the birds.

I went back into the bedroom and pulled the radio out of the pack. I brought it out on to the verandah before calling the ship.

This time I got Pete, and I gave him a quick report on the situation.

"Any idea what's going on there?" he asked, laconically.

"Not yet," I said. "He's as talkative as the other one. But I haven't started yet. He doesn't know that Mme. Levasseur has talked to us, or that she asked us to photograph the region. I did mention the photographs but his eyes didn't light up. The aliens are weird. He appears to be keeping and treating them like some kind of domestic animal. He's taught them to respond to English, and they obviously understand it pretty well from the way he organized getting Nathan out of the pit. But they don't make any sound themselves. It's as though he were talking to superintelligent sheepdogs. They do as they're told and not much else. He says they're completely docile—won't even fight when attacked, despite the fact that some local predator has them singled out as easy meat. I'm not sure what the hell goes on."

"What are you going to do now?"

"Persuade Gley to bring us back to the ship, if I can. He has donkeys, and I think we could do it in a day if we were riding. Nathan's leg needs attention in the lab if we're to reknit the bone and make good the tissue-repair so as to get him on his feet within a week."

"You think he'll do that?"

"I think so. He's more interested in us than he'll let himself show. This cabin's not a recent erection. I think he's been looking for whatever it is he's looking for over a period of years. If we can help him, he'll take the help, though he might not want us in on the hunt."

There wasn't much else to say, and I signed off. There was still no sign of activity beyond the strand of trees.

I got down from the verandah and began to wander around the cabin—not really going anywhere but just seeing what there was to see. Round the back there was a patch of land that was full of flowering plants. It was obvious that it wasn't nature that had crowded so many together so close. Although the ground had never been dug over, and there was no regular pattern at all, I concluded that this was a kind of garden. Gley had brought seeds here from all over the crater and scattered them on this plot to grow up together in anarchic confusion.

There were corollae of all shapes and sizes—again the dominant color was blue, but again all others were represented in some measure. Buzzing insects were everywhere.

"Utopia for bees," I muttered, as my eye passed slowly over the floral display. I noted that a lot of the leaves were scarred with brown patches and that some of the blooms were shriveling.

"Also paradise for plant parasites," I said to myself. "And it hasn't been watered for a week. Not since the last rain fell, I'll bet."

I stepped closer to examine some of the more exotic specimens, and it was some time before I passed on to the more abundant species. It wasn't until I began to look at those that I realised something slightly odd. There were a great number of different species, many of which were obviously closely related. In particular I noticed a number of forms that were giant varieties of others—new species generated by spontaneous polyploidy. There seemed to be *too much* variation. I wondered whether it was an illusion created by the fact that plants from many different areas had been gathered here.

I didn't notice Gley until he was actually standing beside me.

"Admiring my garden?" he asked.

"That's right," I told him.

"You were looking at them very intently. You're a biologist of sorts?"

I had told him about the lab on the ship but I hadn't specified my own role on the mission in talking to him the previous night.

"Of sorts," I agreed.

"So am I," he said, surprisingly. I met his eyes, and showed my surprise as I stared at him.

"There's too much variation," he said. "All these species grow within the crater. A lot of them don't grow outside. At some time in the past there was a burst of evolutionary fervor here, Mr. Alexander. But I don't know how long ago. What do you make of that?"

His voice was more gentle now than it had been the night before, but it was still coarse enough for there to be an apparent dissonance between what he said and the way he said it.

"I don't know," I said, warily. "What does it mean to you?"

He was content to stare at me for a moment.

"I don't know either," he said, eventually—probably lying in his teeth. "The thought of radioactivity had crossed my mind. But it must have been some time ago if there ever was any unusual radioactivity in the soil. There's no sign of tissue damage in the plants. And I've been coming up here for the summer for five years, with at least fifty Sets each time. Neither I nor any of the Sets have shown any symptoms of radiation poisoning. I suppose you could confirm that for me, with the equipment on your ship?"

"Yes," I said. "We could. If there *is* a radiation hazard here we should be able to spot it."

"And I suppose the same equipment could be used for more refined measurements?" he said. "Something along the lines of radiocarbon dating?"

I didn't bother to hide my astonishment. "Radiocarbon dating?" I repeated.

"I was thinking last night," he said. "About what you told me. Your ship coming here to help us sort out any problems of adaptation. I have a small problem. I don't know whether it would help, but if I had some apparatus for making very accurate measurements of radioactivity and some standard analytical apparatus I might be able to glean a few clues."

"What do you want to date?" I asked.

"If there *was* radioactive substance in the soil," he said, "we might be able to find out how long ago it was active . . . by finding out how the amount of radioactive substance left compares to the quantities of the decay products."

"Well," I said, dubiously, "it depends . . . but I guess we could try. I think Linda Beck—she's one of my staff—knows a good deal about radioactive dating. She worked with me in the Latin States for a few months some time before we were attached to the *Daedalus*. She was doing some paleobotanic work then in support of my studies in evolutionary ecology."

I used the jargon deliberately, testing out his claim that he was a biologist "of sorts." He didn't flinch under fire.

"Thank you," he said.

"If you could help me to get Nathan back to the *Daedalus*," I said "we could pick up the equipment then. Perhaps Linda and I could come back with you."

"It's not going to be easy transporting your friend back across the mountain," he said. "But half a dozen Sets working in shifts can do it. If we take eight pack animals we should make a reasonable pace. If we start within the hour we might make it soon after dark."

I frowned. It wasn't that I wanted to object—I was just startled by his sudden hurry.

"Isn't it rather late?" I asked, looking up at the sun.

"The Sets are mountain-bred," he told me. "They're used to the air. And so am I—we've been up here the last couple of months. We'll do the fifty miles a good deal quicker than you did. It's not as if there was any real climbing involved—only gentle slopes."

"It is mostly a matter of crossing a shallow valley and the tableland," I agreed. "Do we have time to eat first?"

"The Sets are getting things ready," he said. "And they're cooking some food. You'll need a solid hot meal to set you both up for the trip."

He led the way back round the side of the cabin to the verandah and the door. I wondered quickly about the significance of these new revelations. The fact that he was a biologist changed my whole perspective on the puzzle of what he was doing up here. I'd spent a lot of time in regions just as remote, and suddenly he seemed not so much an anti-social lunatic looking for some mythical goal on the imaginative level of the Fountain of Youth but an honest intellectual motivated by curiosity and perhaps directed by some arcane ecological problem of the kind we had come to help sort out. It was a change of image that made for a much nicer story, but somehow it just didn't seem to fit.

As I stepped up on to the verandah there came a quivering sensation which made me reach out and grip the portal. For a second or two I thought it was something inside me making me shiver, but as the sensation went on and grew in magnitude I realized that the verandah was creaking slightly as it shook. In fact, the very earth was shaking.

I grabbed the portal hard, with terror welling up inside me as I realized what the tremor was, and I turned to Gley with my panic written all over my face. But he was standing quite unconcerned, not even bothering to seek support.

My terror was displaced by an eccentric anger at his composure. He wasn't laughing at me but I felt that I was making a complete fool of myself.

"It's all right," he said. "It happens quite often."

Even while he spoke the tremor was dying—passing on without having had any real effect on the cabin. I was almost relieved to hear a couple of crashes as it passed on. A cup had fallen off a shelf and a stack of pans had collapsed.

I swallowed hard. "How often?" I asked.

"About twice a week," he said, in an off-hand manner. "Mostly they're no worse than that. Occasionally we get a big one that rattles the teeth a bit. But the crater's bedrock is quite firm—lava originally, of course. The surface cracks a little, and the vents at the north end tend to grow a bit wider and blow off some noxious gas, but there's absolutely no danger to life and limb. There's no loose rock on this face of the mountain to slide into the crater, even if a feeble shaking like that could start it."

"What about the local volcanoes?" I asked. "You're in the middle of three of them."

"Quite extinct," he assured me. "The whole range is

inactive. I guess there are still pressure-spots deep down, but they release their tension in little tremors. They're the last twitches of something long dead."

I wasn't convinced by his confidence. "You built a house here?" I croaked. "And you come up here every summer to spend your time in a place that averages two earthquakes a week?"

He grinned. It was the first time I'd seen him smile. His face was wide enough to give it astonishing dimension.

"You get used to it," he said.

"No doubt," I observed. "But *why*?"

"I own the mountains," he said, the grin disappearing. "I guess I own the earthquakes too."

"Congratulations," I said, not knowing how I'd touched the nerve that had wiped the smile off his face. I thought that it might be a good idea to steer the conversation back to safer ground, and was casting around for a nice neutral comment when I heard Nathan call out: "Alex!"

The tremor had woken him up, and must have thrown him into just as much of a panic as it had thrown me. I went through quickly to reassure him that it only happened twice a week and it never did any serious damage. After I'd reconciled him to this fact I thought it wise to call the ship as well, just in case they were consumed by desperate fears.

"Did you feel the tremor?" I said to Pete.

"What tremor?" he replied.

"We just had an earthquake."

"We didn't."

Fifty miles, I thought, is a long way. Presumably we were near—or even above—the epicentre.

"Apparently," I said, "there are two a week. But most of them are little ones. I guess you won't feel it unless we get a slightly bigger one . . . or unless one starts closer to you."

"Thanks for the warning," he said, sounding very bored by the matter.

"You're welcome. And by the way, we're coming home. Starting within the hour. Rumor has it the Sets are capable of prodigious stamina, so we'll be with you about nightfall, or soon after."

"Okay," he replied. I signed off.

I went back to see Gley, who was in the main room with a couple of Sets, supervising the cooking.

"With our luck running the way it is at present," I said, "this entire mountainside could split itself open just for the pleasure of swallowing us up."

"It won't," he assured me. But he said it quite flatly, in a voice which seemed to lack conviction.

Johann Gley wasn't by any means the most reassuring person I had ever met. In fact, without even trying, he could be quite unsettling.

7

Getting Nathan back to the *Daedalus* wasn't exactly a joy ride, but it was a great deal easier than I might have imagined. The six-Set stretcher-bearing team picked up the art in no time and they strode out willingly in two-hour shifts while the relief crews rested on donkey-back. We took eight donkeys in all, two for use as pack animals. They were sturdy creatures, and these particular animals were local to the region. They were sure of foot on the slopes and maintained a steady walk hour after hour. They were also fairly comfortable to ride, provided one sat far enough back. They were way ahead of Floria's giant horses on just about every count.

To begin with Gley didn't seem to be in the mood for talk. He had to stay close to the Sets until he was sure that they knew what they were doing and that the task had been thoroughly routinized. As I watched him I was struck again by the analogy of a shepherd working with highly trained dogs. The Sets were clever, but in the sense that a police dog or a guide dog is clever. All the complexity of their behavior was involved with their reactions to Gley and their relationship with him. They took very little notice of one another. There was a rapport between Set and human but none, it seemed, between Set and Set—none, at any rate, that was more sophisticated than the rapport between members of an animal herd.

And yet—the survey team had classified the Sets as intelligent indigenes. Why?

I hadn't really thought about it before. I had just taken the word of the men on the ground, even though I knew that they had done little more than watch the Sets from a distance. They had noted that the Sets appeared to have no technology, but that they occasionally improvised tools in food-gathering which were abandoned and forgotten once the task at hand was forgotten. They had noted that the Sets appeared to have only a rudimentary language, consisting of a dozen or so grunts and cries which were expressive rather than denotative. Even animals on Earth could match that with no trouble. The survey team had called them intelligent because of three things, two of which were really quite meaningless. First, they were humanoid. Second, they had hands with opposable thumbs. Third, they showed a good deal of ingenuity and a degree of cooperation in the business of evading predators. Sometimes one would act as decoy in order to allow others to escape. They would exploit the weaknesses of individual predators, adapting their strategies to particular species and particular circumstances—though always the end was escape and nothing more. They never fought back. They never acted aggressively toward any animal greater than a fly.

Of the three factors, the second and the third were insignificant. Animals may develop opposable thumbs for gripping, especially if they live in an arboreal environment. Lots of prey species develop sophisticated strategies of evasion, often on a group basis involving "altruistic" behavior. But that the Sets were humanoid was something else. An upright stance is mechanically unsound. It doesn't evolve unless there are very strong selective compensations. It frees the hands for manipulative work, but that isn't enough. Its the hand *in association with the large brain* that really offers the potential for intelligence and intelligent control of the environment. The Sets had large brains. They walked upright. They were considerably more humanoid than a chimpanzee. They had everything they needed in order to develop a highly sophisticated intelligence and control of the environment.

But they hadn't.

The survey team had been presented with an enigma. Perhaps they genuinely had not realized it. Perhaps they had decided to gloss over it. Perhaps they had decided that it was really a non-problem that could be solved without any extensive discussion. But for whatever reason they had arrived at a judgment which now seemed to me to contain a large and dubious assumption.

They had decided that the Sets were intelligent, at least potentially, despite the fact that the concomitants of intelligence—the selective advantages which intelligence confers and which thus provide its evolutionary *raison d'être*—were absent. They had blithely assumed that it is possible to have intelligence and not to use it. But what *is* intelligence if not intelligence *in use*? And at a more trivial level, how can one ever assert that someone else is intelligent if one never sees him behaving intelligently? What possible meaning can there be in such an assertion?

The Sets, it seemed to me, were not intelligent. They were clever, and marvelously adaptable. They could be trained to a number of very complex manipulative tasks. But they were *not* intelligent, in any fashion analogous to the intelligence of human beings. They were animals—perhaps the ultimate in domestic animals.

Which was all very well as a judgment. Fine—survey team nil, Alex one. But it certainly didn't get rid of the enigma. If the survey team had been wrong in calling the Sets intelligent because they were humanoid, and they were really unintelligent, then *why were they humanoid*? Physical forms don't evolve by accident. They evolve under selective pressure. What possible selective pressure could reproduce the human form so completely while having no connection with the actual selective pressures that on Earth had moulded the human form? I was an upright biped because my remote ancestors had needed a spiral column to support a big brain and the big skull to wrap around it, and because they needed their hands free to make and build things, thus cementing a positive feedback loop by which the better their brains became the more things they could do, and the more things they could do the more complex the brain had to be. Man made tools, and tools made man.

Only the Sets hadn't made tools. What, then, made the Sets?

It was quite a paradox. The colonists could perceive it too. Helene Levasseur knew about it, and so did Gley. Helene Levasseur wanted aerial photographs of the Isis mountains. One of the things that shows up well on aerial photographs is land that was once—no matter how long ago—brought under cultivation. The Isis mountains were just about dead center of the Sets' natural range. Gley wanted radioactive dating equipment, to find out how long ago some mysterious source of radiation (at present quite hypothetical) had originated in that curious elliptical crater.

Maybe they both believed that once—long, long ago—the Sets *had* made tools, and had been made *by* them. Maybe they had had agriculture, even civilization. But they did not have them now.

It was one way out of the paradox—perhaps the only way. It was at least conceivable that the Sets had *had* intelligence to go with the humanoid form which was one of its symptoms, but that something had happened to take it all away from them: civilization, agriculture, tool-using, and intelligence itself. Something had destroyed the capabilities that evolution had built.

If that *were* the hypothesis that Gley and Mme. Levasseur were working with it was easy to see the cause of their anxiety. If such a thing *had* happened to the Sets—and in all probability they were still looking hard for proof that it *had*—then they had to know what had caused it. Just in case there was the possibility—however remote—that it might happen to them, too.

I was mulling over this chain of thought, vaguely dissatisfied with it but for the moment unable to form any other hypothesis which took care of all the puzzling facts, when Gley came abreast of me.

"That radio set," he said. "I remembered something. There's a town out to the east of the mountains . . . close to the farm where I spend the winter. They have some of the communications apparatus that came out with the colony ships in the year dot. Some of it was preserved, in case Earth managed to send out support ships or more colony ships. I don't suppose it's in working order after all this time. . . ."

There was a question lurking in the speculation.

"It's working," I confirmed. "We spoke to the people on the ground. We were trying to land somewhere near the town."

"Ah." He nodded. I could see that the train of thought was still chugging on inside his head, but I figured that I had no real interest in seeing where it would stop next.

"You spend the winter on a farm, then?" I said, asking subtly for amplification.

"I work during the winter," he said. "There's a good deal of work that Sets can't do—or can only do badly—but there aren't many people willing to work. There's always pressure on the farming families because they have to supervise the Sets *and* do a lot of the more complicated jobs. Supervising Sets is a skill, but even when you've mastered it it takes up a lot of time. They're always glad to take me on, even if the main farm business is already finished. They can't get anyone else—everyone wants to gather his own herd of Sets and work his own land . . . except for the people in the government."

"What about industries?"

He shrugged. "Same as the farms. Everyone wants to rule his own little empire. The Sets are the workforce, the supervision is usually a family affair. There are partnerships and groups forming all the time among the younger people, but they break up in their own good time when the element of cooperation's no longer vital. Only family units have any real sticking power. Mind you, with people scattered the way they are family units grow large. Three or four generations together. It's only the minority that leave to start their own concerns, though there'd probably be a lot more if it weren't for government policy with land leases. By slowing down the legal machinery they keep the rate at which new concerns open up under control, and hold families and existing partnerships together longer than some of them would like. Maybe that's good in some respects, because a lot of farms and industrial concerns would fold up if they split too soon, but it also gives the government opportunities to show a lot of favor in leases. They tend to look after their own—there's a lot of looking after the family and old-fashioned barter. But that's the way it is."

He sounded bitter about it. I presumed that his own career hadn't quite gone as he'd wished. But I left that aside for the time being.

"How many Sets are there working on an average farm?" I asked.

"Don't know about the average," he said. "One where I work has six or eight hundred and growing. Some are bigger, especially here and Imhotep, where there were a lot of Sets to start with. Out west, where the colony began, there are more people and fewer Sets. But they breed fast, and Imhotep's exporting a lot now. There's a limit to the number any one man can handle—they have to be shown things, given special orders. Everything has to be checked. They aren't people, you know. They aren't slaves. Or at least, if you call them that it isn't what you'd normally mean by the word. I don't know what you'd call them."

"Domestic animals?" I suggested.

Surprisingly, he shook his head. "They aren't that either. You don't know how it is. We brought livestock from Earth—pigs, chickens, goats—and we've made herd animals out of some things we found here. We have local

animals we call dogs, and ones we call donkeys. *They're*
domestic. But a domestic animal you control completely.
It's purely a matter of use. You can beat 'em, slaughter
'em for food . . . whatever you want. But it isn't that way
with Sets. You can't beat 'em . . . you can't even threaten
'em. If you do, they disappear. The one thing Sets are
good for is work, and to get them to work you have to
treat them the way they expect to be treated. They expect
food, they expect protection. It's not that they want
special rewards, or anything like that—they'll do what
you want as long as you go about it *right*. But threats and
mistreatment they won't take. You can't compel a Set.
You can hurt them and you can kill them but you can't
force them. See?"

"Not entirely," I said, "but I get the general drift. What
I don't quite see is the logic of it all."

"I don't know that there is any," he said. "I don't
know whether it's true or not, with it happening so long
ago, but the way it's told the colony didn't start out with
the intention of making the Sets into what they are now.
People went out to talk to them, to try and be friends
with them—only they can't talk, of course. It was while
they were trying to teach the Sets language in the hope of
talking to them that they discovered the way Sets would
do as they were told. They took it as a sign of intelligence
in the beginning, but it wasn't that. The way it's told the
Sets took to being workers like ducks to water. It was as
if they'd been given an opportunity they'd been waiting
for all their lives and all through their history. When they
found out how easy it was a lot of people became Set-
trainers, and most of them left the colony altogether to set
up on their own, because it was declared illegal at first.
The government fought it, but life wasn't so easy that the
colonists could look a gift horse in the mouth. A new government came in and a new set of laws was designed. The
colony changed its mind and its aims and its methods.
There was a lot in those laws that seemed sensible at the

time, when we were adapting to the new situation, but the
system doesn't seem so good today. All the advantages
have been milked, and it's the flaws that show up now.
With our population multiplied a thousandfold because of
the Sets it seemed reasonable to start giving out massive
land-leases to everyone who wanted to farm. They pack-
aged up almost all the arable land in two continents and
leased it in a matter of years, and the control of the leases
became the key to real power here on Geb. The government owns nothing but the power to manipulate and re-
distribute those leases, but that's become the most
important power there is. Because people can lose the
land they work or the mines they operate or the factories
they run, the men in government have leverage which
compels the support that keeps them in power."

"But you said that you *own* the mountains?" I said.

"Oh sure," he replied. "Not all land is classified as
leasable. The policy's not uniform because there were always people who wanted something that couldn't be taken
away, and it was easier to buy them off one by one than
to let them form a party in opposition to the lease system.
There are islands strung out across the Mediterranean
Sea, and land that's supposedly useless. My grandfather
once had a good lease, but he was squeezed out. My father practically went to war, but there's not a lot one man
can do. He had a couple of hundred Sets, but Sets are
useless in wars. They won't fight. In the end he got
ownership. They wanted to give him an island a thousand
miles from the nearest port, but he wanted the mountains.
Not all of them, of course—just an area of land between
the three volcanoes. At first he intended to farm it, but he
couldn't even get that notion off the ground. He was already too old. He was killed in an accident—not up here,
in Cleopatra. I went to work . . . not for the government
but for an independent concern. Agriculture and technology were sewn up too tightly. We went into biological
research, aiming at the knowledge that would give us bet-

ter control over Geb's environments, better ways of exploiting them. But the government decided they wanted total control over that kind of work. We couldn't get the equipment we needed. We kept going for a long time, but eventually they squeezed the life out of us—absorbed part of the operation and scattered the rest. I still owned the mountains, and I came to believe that they might be interesting—and maybe exploitable—on their own account. They're the center of the Sets' range . . . and when you come to look at it they're the center of one or two other things as well."

"What, exactly, are you looking for?" I asked, feeling that now was the time he might be prepared to tell me. He was unburdening himself of his troubles, and he was in the mood to run on a bit.

"Exactly?" he queried. "If I knew *exactly* I'd have to know a lot more already than I do. I don't know at all. But there's something very curious about that crater. I need to know more before I can begin to guess what I might actually find."

He was deliberately beating about the bush. He wanted to talk but he didn't want to say very much. He didn't yet know whether I was an ally or an enemy. He didn't yet know how much help I could give him or what the price might be. He didn't know whether he wanted to use me or get rid of me.

"When you spoke to the people at Ptolemy," he said, "who was it? And what did they say?" His curiosity on that point had been nagging away at him since the beginning of the conversation.

"A woman named Helene Levasseur," I told him, thinking it was time to lay a card or two on the table.

"Helene Levasseur!" He seemed far more surprised than I'd expected—alarmed, in fact.

"Why?" I asked. "Who is she?"

"Nominally, she's a judge. Actually, she's one of the people that runs Geb. A policy-maker."

"You know her, I suppose?"

"We've never met. But she made the policy that got me exiled to the mountains. It was her idea to bring biological research under the government wing. She was the one who got worried in case we found something. What was she doing in Ptolemy?"

"She didn't say. In fact, she didn't say very much at all. But she's interested in you, and in what you're doing."

"She said so?"

"We deduced it. She asked us to take aerial photographs of the region."

His face went dark, then. He was angry, and for a moment I thought he was angry at me. But it passed quickly.

"What does she expect to learn from those?" he asked.

"I don't know. I was hoping you might be able to explain."

"No," he said, "unless. . . ."

He stopped, leaving me screaming internally in frustration.

"Unless what?" I asked.

But another thought had already displaced it. "Is she coming here?" he asked. "If you gave her your position when you crashed. . . ."

"Yes."

He looked at me long and hard—which is not an easy thing to do when you're bouncing along on the hindquarters of a donkey, looking at someone who's bouncing out of phase on a different donkey.

"I'm not on anyone's side," I assured him. "But I really would like to know what's behind it all."

"You can tell her," he said, ominously, "that she'd better stay on her own side of this valley. My territory ends somewhere up on that saddle. If she comes near the crater, there'll be trouble."

"It's not easy for one man to conduct a war," I reminded him. "You said so yourself."

"That's my business."

"Do you want to look at the aerial photographs?" I asked.

"No," he said. "There's nothing there. I may not know much but I know *that*. I've been combing the ground for five summers. If there'd been anything, I would have found it. I don't know why there isn't anything there, but there isn't."

"No ruins," I said, feeling that it was about time I started throwing out a line. "No sign that there ever was any kind of civilization there. Not even the slightest trace of agricultural development."

He looked me straight in the eye, and simply said: "Not a trace."

8

The operation on Nathan's leg went smoothly, and was over in less than an hour. The level of concentration required for such work, however, is such that even a brief session can leave you exhausted. It's not the amount of energy you have to burn up, it's the mental gear you have to change down from when it's done.

When we were finished and Nathan had been moved back to the bunk in his own cabin I let Linda show Gley over the lab. It was basically a goodwill gesture in the hope of getting him to loosen up still further and tell me the whole story. I already had an uncomfortable feeling, though, that there was no *whole* story to tell—only a lot of little bits that he could no more put together than I could. He was operating on some idea of what may or may not have happened in these parts a long time ago, but he was reluctant to spill it. There was more to his reluctance than the simple strategy of playing his cards close to his chest. His idea was ill-formed, in all likelihood, and maybe more than a little incredible. And on top of the purely intellectual conditions there were a lot of other things to be taken into account: his resentment of the colony and his own personal history, especially the way the mention of Helene Levasseur's name made him want to spit acid. There probably wasn't a whole story there, either—just an untidy heap of experiences and feelings. He wasn't a crazy man but he was a man used to being alone with his thoughts and his feelings, not having to communicate them to anyone. Locked up inside him like that they didn't have the coherence that often only comes with laborious verbal reworking. Whatever he

wanted to find—whatever he wanted to *know*—he wanted
to keep it to himself, not because of any material profit
there was in the monopoly but simply because he wanted
it to be *his*. Maybe the only kind of revenge that was in
any way possible was for him to know something the
people who'd injured him wanted to stop him from knowing and wanted to know themselves. I could understand
that, and even sympathize. But I wanted to know, too,
and if the information was of any significance for the
colony as a whole . . . well, my priorities went a great
deal further than his.

While Linda was talking to Gley I went to see Mariel.
She'd gone outside to watch the Sets. Contact with aliens
was her part of the mission, and it was something she
took very seriously. With her, it was more than a vocation. Her talent had made her a misfit on Earth—the next
best thing to a hopeless mental case—and coming out to
the colonies to put her ability to constructive use was the
only thing that was saving her talent and her personality.
She was nearly nineteen now. Most talents of that kind
burned out two or three years earlier. She'd worked wonders on Wildeblood, and had even managed to get a good
deal out of a sticky situation on Attica. On the other
worlds, too, her ability to read minds *via* faces had come
in handy. I knew she was going to be disappointed now to
find that there was nothing for her in the alien species.

I could see the dismay as I approached her. She'd tried
to talk to them and failed, and now she was sitting on a
rock nursing her injured knee and just watching them as
they stood with the donkeys, patiently, doing nothing.

"They understand what I say," she told me. "I can tell
them to do things and they do. But it's just a *reaction*.
There's no consciousness there that shows in the way they
listen. Their faces are blank . . . there are none of the involuntary signals that go with real communication, nor
even the hesitation that goes with cogitation. They don't
talk to one another. They don't meet one another's gaze.

They glance covertly, just to keep a running check on what the others are doing, but they do it automatically. If you tell one to do something that requires two of them he can't pass on the message. You have to tell both. With a lot of experiments in specific situations I could probably work out the limits of human/alien communication. But is there any point? They're blank."

"Animals," I said. "Just animals."

"Well . . ." she began.

When she stopped, I said, "Well?"

"I'm not sure it's as simple as that. I've met blankness before, remember. Not in animals."

She was talking about Arcadia and the people of the City of the Sun. They had conscious minds all right—but not like ours. They had once been human but they were human no longer. Their faces showed nothing because their mental processes had been disconnected from the simple animal level of communication that still accompanied ours, and through which Mariel gained access to them.

"You think the Sets may be something similar?" I asked.

She shook her head. "No. They're . . . less disturbing than that. With the people of the City, it was as if I were looking into a vacuum, where there *ought* to be something but there wasn't. Here . . . yes, it *is* like looking at an animal, in a way, but. . . . there just aren't words to explain it, Alex. The sensations I get are private to me alone . . . there aren't words to describe it and if there were you couldn't understand them. There aren't even words by which I could attempt to interpret the sensations and discover what they *mean*."

The frustration in her voice took on a note of desperation. I reached out a hand and she took it. I squeezed gently.

"It's okay," I said. "There *is* something weird, but we'll crack it."

"Without my help."

"You're not superhuman," I told her.

"I'm supposed to be," she replied. "It's what I'm here for."

"No," I said. "You're here because you're a human with talents and skills, just like the rest of us. You can't work magic. Do you think *I* don't get sensations I can't put into words? Do you think the rest of us don't have feelings we can't explain or begin to understand? You can't ask for perfection in yourself any more than we can—you can only do so much. You're not a miracle-worker."

She let go my hand, and said, "I know."

"They're just *too* clever," I said. "Too damned handy. All these skills that they've picked up with such facility . . . it just doesn't make sense that the potential should be there and yet so completely untapped. And this business of docility . . . they don't fight, not even when things with teeth and claws jump on them and rip them apart. They're completely non-aggressive, and if they're mistreated they just run away. They're so willing to work, and the crazy thing is that they're not even *greedy*. They expect to be fed and cared for, like pets. And they'll do so much for such trivial rewards. What kind of evolutionary process produced a creature like that? What happened to the struggle for existence and the survival of the fittest? A creature like this just can't exist."

"But they do."

"They do," I agreed. "And somewhere, that means there's an answer. A hidden factor that overcomes all the objections with a single neat stroke."

"Why are they called Sets?" she asked.

"The ancient Egyptians represented their gods as having the heads of animals," I told her. "Theriomorphism. Most of the representations are immediately recognizable—the crocodile, the ibis, the cow, the falcon. Just ordinary animals walking erect, as they do in cartoons and some children's fantasies. But one was an enigma. The god Sutekh, shortened to Seth or Set. He was based on an animal that couldn't be identified. One theory has it that he represents a mythical animal that never did exist—a legendary beast that was the product of an artist's imagination. But how can that be? It seems to break the entire pattern, the whole logical order of their cosmological thought."

I realized even while I said it how apposite it sounded. A creature to break the pattern . . . to defy the preconceptions built into our understanding of the way things happen.

"Go on," said Mariel.

"Sutekh was the god of disorder," I said. "Not an evil god . . . at least, not in the early days of the Egyptian culture. They didn't have the sense of priorities that represents chaos as the ultimate evil. He was the brother of Horus, and they formed a pair—Horus the bright eye of the sun, Set the dark counterpart. Later, though, he became the adversary of Osiris, and the Osirian cult tried to banish him from the pantheon, making him a kind of devil. Mythologies change, you see . . . they evolve just like species. Set was never quite without friends, but he acquired a lot of enemies."

"And what was the animal whose head he had?"

"No one knows for sure. But he also had a rigid upright tail with a forked tuft at the end. The river hog has a tail like that. It's possible that the Set animal was a species of pig that once lived in the Nile valley but became extinct there some time during the first millennium B.C. But no one can say for certain, and in all likelihood no one will ever be able to say for certain. It's a problem that can't be answered, because all the data we have to work with is more than two thousand years out of date."

I wondered how far out of date was the data that Johann Gley had to work with in his enigmatic crater. Maybe that old, or much older. The secret of the Sets might be lost in a past so distant that hardly anything remained at all. Not a trace, Gley had said, of any culture they might once have had, here or anywhere else.

"But these aren't gods," observed Mariel. "They're the very opposite. Creatures whose gods are men."

"I suspect Gley thinks they may be the decadent relic of a culture that disappeared a long time ago."

She pondered the idea for a moment, then shook her head. "No. There'd be more vestiges of what they once were. Not things they once built or things they once did—I can accept all trace of that being wiped out. But there'd be some echo in what they *are*. It may be possible for a species to lose its intelligence and become stupid . . . but not for it to become a complete blank. I can't accept that."

I curled my lip. "I must admit that I arrived at the same notion," I said. "I didn't like it, either . . . but I'm damned if I can think of a better one. Or any other one at all."

"You may yet," she said. "If anyone can, you can."

"Thanks."

"You, too."

I felt slightly embarrassed, and turned away to go back to the ship.

"Alex," she called after me.

I turned.

"I can't read the Sets," she said, "but I can read Gley. He's the kind of man who has a short temper when he's dealing with other people. And he's been seized recently by a sudden sense of urgency."

"It's because he knows that Helene Levasseur is coming here," I said. "He's very possessive about his mountains. Also, he thinks he's in some kind of competition to get the glittering prize of some nugget of information he thinks she wants and is trying to stop him from getting. Does that make sense?"

"Just about," she said. "I thought I'd warn you."

"*Warn* me? Why?"

"Because you're on his side. You always pick your side too easily. And because you're going back to the crater with him tomorrow or the next day. I think he'll try to stop you from finding the solution, too, even if he needs you to help *him* find it."

"Well," I said. "There's another runner for them both to contend with, now. *I'm* in the competition too. May the best man win."

She gave me a half-smile to tell me that she understood, that she disapproved, and that she knew full well there wasn't anything she could do or say. She could read me as easily as she could read herself. Maybe more easily. That went for everybody on the *Daedalus*.

I returned the grin, and went on.

Knowing that fools rush in where angels fear to tread isn't enough to qualify anyone for wings and a halo.

9

We gave Gley a cabin, feeling that it was the least we could do in view of his own generous hospitality. We also fed him. Though none were voiced, opinions apparently varied as to whether the good, nourishing concentrates we offered him were preferable to the rather more primitive fare he had provided for us. The Sets had brought along a dismantled tepee on the back of one of the pack animals, and they pitched this outside.

Helene Levasseur called the ship in the late evening to assure us that she was steadily making progress. Karen reported that we'd made contact with Gley and that he'd helped us out after the accident, but diplomatically didn't mention that he was standing in the doorway listening to every word that was said. Mme. Levasseur didn't seem rapturous about the idea of our having talked to Gley, but she didn't want to talk about it. She was a very cautious person, as befitted a judge with an interest in politics. I was strongly tempted to displace Karen for a few moments so that I could tell her that Gley wanted it passed on (a) that there could be nothing worth looking at on the photographs and (b) that he intended to shoot her if she set foot in his crater, but I refrained. Common sense held unchallenged sway over the proceedings.

When I showed Gley to his cabin I was careful to point out the shower and offer him some clean clothes. He was uninterested in the latter, but I was glad when he took a constructive attitude to the former. I was about to leave him to it when I noticed that he had something else on his mind.

"Do you have spacesuits on board?" he asked.

I couldn't help dropping my jaw just a little.

"Spacesuits?" I echoed. Then, seeing that he was waiting for an answer, I added, "No."

"But you have something," he went on, quickly. "The girl mentioned it. Suits to maintain sterile conditions, with air filters."

"We have sterile suits," I agreed. "But they're just glorified plastic bags. The filters take out all the organic matter from the air, and some obnoxious gases, but they can strain water, and you can squeeze liquefied food through the filters too. They certainly wouldn't do for wandering about in space."

"I don't want to wander about in space," he said. "Rather the reverse."

For a moment I was at a loss to see what he meant. Then I got it.

"The cracks in the northern wall of the crater," I said. "You want to go pot-holing on the side of a volcano. Why the suits?"

"Sulphur dioxide," he said. "Not much of it, but enough to make it very dangerous to go down there for any length of time. And the water vapor that belches out occasionally can be hot."

"The filters will stop SO_2," I said, dubiously. "And the suits have an air-system to which we can attach oxygen bottles if they begin to fail. Hot vapor might still be a problem, though."

"It's just a matter of keeping it off the skin," he said.

"There is a thermostatic control of sorts," I told him. "But it was designed with cold in mind rather than heat. I don't know that the water recycler would appreciate working at high temperatures."

"I'll take the risk," he said.

"Why? Why the hell would you want to go into the fissures?"

"That's my business," he said. "You don't have to come along. Just give me a suit."

"First you want to borrow equipment for measuring radioactivity," I said, "now you want a sterile suit. And you won't say a damn thing about the theory you're working on. What could possibly be inside the mountain?"

"You're a clever man Mr. Alexander," he said. "You can work it out for yourself."

They say it takes two to make a competition. He appeared to have read my character right, if what he said really was a challenge. But maybe he was just stalling in a faintly insulting way.

"You can have the suit," I said. "When do you want to go back?"

"There isn't much time," he said. "I don't want to hang about here waiting for Helene Levasseur. I'm going back tomorrow."

"That'll be the third time in three days I've traveled that fifty miles."

"You don't have to come."

"I'd like to take another look at your garden. Anyhow, you'll need at least one of us to operate the radiation apparatus."

He shrugged.

I left him to get on with his shower. I went straight to Linda's cabin, but she wasn't there. I found her in the lab.

She had already sorted out such equipment as we had for making sensitive radiation counts. She was working now with the light microscope, looking at sections she'd cut from various types of plant fiber.

"What are you doing that for?" I asked. "That's routine drudge-work."

"I cut the sections to see if I could get radio-carbon counts," she explained. "Just a matter of testing the apparatus. They register, but the counts are very low and quite stable. They're exactly what one would expect, given the radio-carbon count in the atmosphere."

"It's no surprise," I said. "But why the microscope?"

"Since I had the sections I thought I might as well take

a look," she replied. "Pity to waste them. Besides, I'm looking for something."

"Don't *you* start," I groaned. "Just because everyone else is operating a triple-locked memory bank there's no need for us to start."

"It's no secret," she assured me. "It's in the survey report in black and white. Quite unimportant. Just curiosity. You know."

I did know. A survey report is just page after page of words and figures. Comprehensive chaos. Everything you ever wanted to know about Geb was there, encoded into quantified data. It was all good solid *knowledge,* but it didn't represent understanding. You can look at words and figures until they begin to swim before your eyes, but they never *really* start to mean anything until you get to the world and start looking at things. A picture is worth a thousand words, they say. A visual image can make a whole page of information clear and coherent. You can't know reality from printed pages—only a particular kind of abstract from reality. To get to know reality you have to see it and touch it and cut it up into little sections to inspect it under a microscope. There's a great deal that can't be condensed into quantified data—sometimes everything that matters.

I found the survey report on the table, open at a page which dealt with some tortuously detailed analysis of the chemical basis of life on Geb. It was work that had taken years to do, based not on the brief time the team had spent here but on the follow-up investigation they'd done in the lunar labs of plant and animal specimens brought back from the world. The page dealt with one of the curious—but by no means unique—features of Geb lifesystem.

Most life-systems only have one basic system of genetic information-transfer—one species of chemical molecule that carries a genetic code. Earth's basic species is the nucleic acids, of which there are two natural varieties and half a dozen artificial forms used in genetic engineering. Most Earthlike worlds thus far investigated have between one and four varieties of a single basic species, but one or two have rather more diverse systems in which three or four varieties of molecules from two distinct species are represented. This is presumably the result of two life-systems evolving independently in the primordial oceans and only later becoming integrated into a single land life-system. The situation is much more common on less Earthlike worlds because of their different biotic characters—it is, in fact, one major cause of unsuitable biotic characters on worlds that are potentially Earthlike but actually unsuitable for colonization.

Geb was a world of the rare kind that is chemically highly compatible with Earth life and yet has more than one species of nucleic acid-analogue. In fact it had two different species each with three common varieties. Metazoan and complex plant life were each "mixed" in the sense that one variety of each species was represented there.

"You're looking at the cell structure of plants which use different species of coding molecules?" I asked.

"That's right," she confirmed.

"Is there a particular reason?"

"Not really. But I had the sections and I wanted to look at something, and it seemed like the most interesting thing to look at. Only it isn't, very. The difference isn't by any means striking."

"It wouldn't be," I said. "The different systems would have met quite early in their evolutionary careers. Under normal circumstances one would have outcompeted the other and survived alone, but these two managed to co-adapt. They've been a major selective factor in one another's development. In many cases, even at the most basic level—in fact, *especially* at the most basic level—the price of coexistence has been convergent evolution. In order that both should survive they had to become very similar. And when it came to metazoan evolution that meant building the same kinds of metazoan reproductive machines. The differences in cell structure are bound to be subtle."

I wondered, carelessly, whether this might be linked with the high rate of variation in the crater. I imagined a situation where there were two different coding molecules, each one manufacturing molecules that were mutagenic with respect to the other—a kind of basic competitive stratagem which had led not to the elimination of one species by the other but to the rapid evolution of both. It was a fascinating theme, but one of no real relevance to the other problems on my mind.

I peered over her shoulder until she moved aside and let me look down the microscope. She switched the slides for me and told me which was which.

"You're right," I said. "Nothing spectacular. Something to ponder deeply on a rainy day. We'll have lots of time. Especially if we're stuck up here the entire time we're on the planet."

"Okay," she said. "We might as well get some sleep. You must be exhausted."

"You've no idea," I told her, "and by the way, we're starting out early in the morning."

"Who's *we*?"

"You, me and Gley. We take the radiation equipment, and three sterile suits."

"Sterile suits?" she said, warily.

"Just in case we fancy a journey to the center of the planet," I said. "Didn't you know that there are always exciting subterranean worlds under volcanoes?"

"I didn't know we were planning to visit one."

"Gley is," I told her.

"*Three* suits?"

"Well, you never know," I said. "He may want some radiation counts made while he's down there."

"You're crazy," she said.

I hadn't the nerve to deny it. I went to bed.

❀ 10 ❀

It is an oft-repeated lie that many significant discoveries have been made in sleep. People confronted with problems of tortuous complexity, it is said, worry themselves to the point of nervous breakdown and then exile themselves to the land of dreams, letting their subconscious common sense, thus unfettered, get down to the job of tying all the loose ends together. They wake up both refreshed and wiser.

Unlike many oft-repeated lies this one has at least the shadow of a truth among its implications. The power of conscious rational thought—immense though it is—is only a means of *processing* ideas. It *tests* them, helping us to sort out the true from the false by making hypotheses jump through hoops. Consciousness worries our notions like a dog worrying a rat, ultimately dragging the entrails from them and exposing any unwilling *reductio ad absurdum* that may be lurking therein, concealed from immediate perception by a gaudy spray of rhetoric. But conscious rational thought is in this sense no more than prophylactic. It protects us, in some measure, from error. It helps us check up on the notions created in the imagination by investigating their internal consistency and comparing them with what we know of the world. Conscious rational thought, however, does not in itself *produce* hypotheses. The so-called process of induction in which Francis Bacon invested so much of his faith in perfect science and the prospect of a better world is not genuinely creative of ideas. Sometimes, it is true, a knowledge of the data may touch hidden springs in the mind which releases hypothe-

ses, but it is from secret places in the caverns of the mind
that notions are actually generated.

Or to put it another way, you can pound your brain all
day and come up with nothing if it so happens that all the
ideas you are disembowelling are the wrong ones. Sometimes having your head full of bad ideas will prevent you
from realizing that there are others you haven't even
thought of.

But in the sleep of reason, so we are assured, nightmares come. And with nightmares (though we so often
fail to see this because the emotions stirred by the dream
capture our attention so completely) come notions. They
are thrust up from the unconscious, and might *just* be
caught and held, if only consciousness can come upon
them, invading the dream with tigerish ease to grab them
in its claws. Sometimes, it happens.

All the real work still needs to be done, in wakefulness—the testing, the teasing, the worrying.

Most of the great hypotheses of history emerged during
wakefulness and were captured then—but the process
which generated them (as opposed to the process which
tested them) is active in sleep as well as in wakefulness,
and hence the myth. Sometimes in sleep you *can* find a
new notion which may strike consciousness with all the
impact of inspiration.

And so, I think, it was that I awoke the next morning
with something in my mind that had not been there when
I went to sleep—an idea grown awesome and bloated in
the few fleeting seconds between sleep and alertness,
where my persona discovered it, interpreted it and understood it.

A less phlegmatic man might have been tempted to cry
"Eureka!" but it is a habit I have grown out of. Ideas
which provoke such a reaction always seem red hot when
you first encounter them, but what matters is how they
check out. I was very wary of this one, first because it

was so unlikely, and second because if it was true it was
an idea with some very far-reaching implications.

I got down to some hard conscious, rational thinking to
test it out against everything I knew already—not an easy
thing to do before breakfast.

The new idea was not dispelled. It grew and grew, and
came to seem the only explanation which fit all the facts.
That, of course, was an illusion. There are always lots of
explanations which fit the facts, and if the one you're
working on seems to fit them better than the rest, that's
just as likely to be due to the fact that it's the one
presently occupying your mind as to the fact that it's the
right one.

I felt, intuitively, that I was right. But I knew this was
one intuition that would have to take some very rigorous
examination, because it wasn't one to blurt out. If true, it
put our whole mission in a new perspective. And if it was
the hypothesis that Gley and Mme. Levasseur were working with, I could understand their reluctance to start
shouting it from the rooftops—especially in our direction.
At breakfast, I didn't mention it to anyone—not because
I was jealous of my proprietary rights or because I
thought it best to keep the dread secret away from such
delicate ears as Mariel's or Conrad's, but because I wanted
to be careful. If necessary, I decided, I would talk it over
with Gley—once I was sure that his idea of what had
happened some time in the near or distant past was the
same as mine. Linda could referee, or perhaps play devil's
advocate.

After we'd eaten I went back to the lab to check the
survey report. The information I wanted wasn't in the
printed version, and I had to get the computer to map it
out for me specially. It only took a few seconds. What I
asked for was the distribution, in terms of number of
known species and in terms of estimated biomass, of the
two species of genetic coding system occurring naturally
on Geb. What I got—in both cases—was a series of con-

tour lines, each one a complex curve like a particularly protean amoeba. They crossed only in a couple of places. For the most part they were stacked inside one another looking for all the world like a great mountain. Its peak was the Isis mountains. That was where the biomass ratio was greatest in favor of one of the two systems—about 70/30. The ratio declined steadily as one went away from the mountains—distorted by other geographical features and interrupted by the bulbous Mediterranean Sea which separated Akhnaton from Imhotep. There were still some places in the antipodean sub-continent, one hundred and eighty degrees removed from the Isis mountains, where the ratio was 0/100.

It was exactly what I would have expected on the basis of my new idea, but it wasn't what any sane man would call proof. Proof—if there *was* any proof accessible to the human hand or eye—was only likely to turn up in or near or underneath the elliptical crater. If Gley was right, and the aerial photographs were useless, then we only had two options open to us—the attempt to discover something by radioactive dating and the attempt to discover something by going into the ground. Left to myself, I'd have advocated digging, slowly and carefully, in the soil of the crater. But I didn't suppose for one moment that Gley would approve of that. He'd been fired with a powerful sense of urgency by the knowledge that Helene Levasseur was coming here—and might just be aware of what he was doing and why—and also by the fact that *we* were here. He wasn't going to settle for an extended archaeological exploration. He wanted action. And sterile suits.

We made rapid preparations to move out. I took a couple of pills to boost my flagging enthusiasm and to help my lungs get more benefit out of the thin air. I offered similar help to Linda, but she refused. She hadn't done any walking yet.

We loaded equipment onto the donkeys—sterile suits, oxygen bottles, tubes of liquefied food and radiation measuring equipment. By the time we'd done it there weren't enough animals for everyone to ride, and the Sets had to take turns walking. They didn't seem to consider this too unreasonable.

Mme. Levasseur checked in with her customary assurances that it wouldn't be long before she reached us. We made suitably neutral noises in return, and didn't even bother to mention that two of us were headed back to the crater with Gley.

Gley led the way, and I was quite happy to lag behind, letting the pack animals and a couple of Sets get between us. I tried not to feel too sick at the thought of yet another day spent traversing the same fifty miles. The scenery had almost ceased to interest me.

Linda, however, came alongside. There was something on her mind.

"You're not really intending to use those suits?" she asked.

"Gley is," I told her, repeating what I'd said the night before.

"And you'll let him?"

"I think so. I might even go with him."

"And me?"

"That's up to you. You're very probably right in thinking that it's insane. Those fissures probably lead nowhere, but if they lead anywhere at all it's not likely to be pleasant. The volcano's inactive, but there's still some rock down there hot enough to blow out steam now and again. And there may be more gas than the filters can protect us from, though they should take care of sulphur dioxide with no trouble."

"Then why go down?"

"I only said that I might."

"Why even think about it?"

I paused, hesitating while I turned over possible replies in my mind. Finally, I said, "Because it's possible that he's right. It's just possible that it's the easiest and quickest way to get to the heart of the matter. *If* there's anything to find. If there isn't . . . the difficulties might begin then. Because he's convinced that he's right, and he's determined to find something that will show him beyond all shadow of a doubt . . . something that he could show to others, if ever he wanted to."

"If he's convinced he's right, but doesn't want to tell anyone, why does he need proof?"

"We all need proof," I said. "No matter how convinced we are, we all keep seeking justification and support . . . continually. The craving doesn't necessarily diminish even when we've found it. Even our most cherished ideas need perpetual reinforcement. *Particularly* our most cherished ideas. Otherwise, how would we maintain our faith in ourselves?"

"But what is he expecting to find?"

"I don't know."

"Come on, Alex—like hell you don't. You *have* to know. Otherwise there'd be no way on Earth you'd even consider the possibility of going into the fissures."

"I've always been known for my recklessness," I said, stalling rather than arguing.

"Alex," she said, intensely, "I want to know. I'm on the expedition. Whether I go with you or not I want to know what game we're playing. Don't you think I have a right to know?"

"Yes," I conceded, "I suppose you do." I was still reluctant, and for more than one reason. It wasn't just that I'd caught the mistrusting disease from Gley. Once, on Arcadia, Nathan had said something that I'd not been able to put out of my mind since. He'd suggested that it wasn't likely that the UN had sent out a mission as prejudiced as ours seemed to be. Officially, we had been sent to help the colonies. Unofficially, Nathan had been commissioned to prepare a case for the reinstitution of the space program. I was also known to be heavily biased in favor of such a reinstitution. According to Nathan the

UN—or factions within the UN—must have commissioned someone else to prepare the opposite case. Whoever was doing so was doing so covertly. For various reasons—mainly the elimination of unlikely suspects—I thought that might be Linda. I'd never said anything, partly because I was half-ashamed of the suspicion, but I'd never quite been able to trust Linda fully with my confidences since I tagged her as the girl most likely.

Now I was caught in something of a tangle. I didn't want to tell her firstly because of my reluctance to put my hypothesis on parade, and partly because I was reluctant to put it on parade *before her*. On the other side, I had a strong feeling that if I was right, and if I could find some kind of clear proof to back up my rightness, then any cases anyone had made so far were all but meaningless.

"You remember what you were looking at last night?" I said, eventually, compromising with my reluctance by adopting an oblique approach.

"Of course I remember," she replied, a distinct note of exasperation creeping into her voice.

"This morning I plotted out the distribution of the two types of coding molecule—the distribution of the two co-adapted life-systems, as it was when the survey team was here. It was pretty rough, of course, because it was based on very scrappy data. But the pattern was remarkably clear. The distribution changes along a fairly steady gradient. One system accounts for nearly three-quarters of the biomass here in the mountains, but is virtually unknown on the other side of the world. What does that suggest to you?"

She didn't want to play guessing games. But she'd known me a long time, and she'd learned to be patient with my little foibles. I got the impression sometimes she thought I was a bit of a pompous fool. I guess she had an arguable case, though I hope she'd have lost in the end.

"That one system—as a system—enjoys a selective advantage in this region while the other enjoys a selective advantage on the other side of the world."

"The Sets belong to the system dominant here."

"Obviously. This is the middle of their range."

"But we don't actually *know* that for certain, because the survey team thought the Sets were intelligent indigenes and hence left them alone. They didn't bring back a specimen for subsequent analytical work."

"They didn't bring back *any* animal larger than a mouse."

"But they dissected others and brought back tissue specimens. Not the Sets."

"Where is all this leading to, Alex? We're going round in tiny circles."

"I think we might find that although the Sets *do* have coding molecules belonging to the species which is dominant hereabouts they'll be a different variety from that of the other metazoan species."

"Why? And so what?"

"It's a prediction," I said. "And it's an unlikely one. Genetic systems are often heterogeneous to some degree at the bacterial level, but almost never at the metazoan level. Agreed?"

"Agreed." Her voice was pregnant with weary patience.

"So if the prediction's right, it's significant—it says a lot in favor of the hypothesis which generated it. Bear that in mind for future reference, because there might be a lot of argument about it at some later stage if Gley doesn't manage to turn up some hard evidence."

"It's on record," she said. "Now for God's sake get on with it."

"We've plenty of time," I assured her. "The key is simply this. Everything we know about the Sets fails to make sense if we try to account for their characteristics in the context of standard evolutionary theory. You haven't seen much of them, but I have—and I checked it all with Mariel last night. The Sets are unintelligent but can be trained to an astonishing level of competence. They're totally docile. They just aren't *self-interested* enough to be accountable in terms of natural selection. They're not aggressive and they're not greedy. I can't accept that as an account of a natural organism. I thought at first that Gley might be nursing a crazy notion about their being the degenerate descendants of a once-civilized species, but the guess was wrong. It took until this morning for me to see the other alternative."

I paused, expectantly. I was almost hoping that given the lead she could produce the answer on cue. I had a silly, perverse feeling that that would somehow let me off the hook. I wouldn't have told her—she'd have come upon the answer herself, independently.

Only she didn't try. She was fed up with games.

All she said was, "So?"

"So they aren't intelligent aliens or unintelligent aliens or products of natural selection. They're androids."

She didn't bother to fall off her donkey in a dead faint. She wasn't melodramatically minded. She didn't even say "Incredible!" She wasn't much of a Dr. Watson either.

"Made by whom?" she asked.

"Colonists," I said. "Colonists who have a slightly better genetic engineering technology than we do. We can already make synthetic nucleic acids—new varieties of the basic species—to set up quasi-living systems and to make viruses. We can't begin to engineer real organisms, but that's really only a single breakthrough away. Once we can make an amoeba we can make an alga or a fish or an android. Already we can modify existing forms of primitive organism by introducing new genes, and we can add to metazoan capabilities with infective viruses. In a hundred years' time . . . or two hundred . . . . we could be making creatures whose bodies *and minds* have been fully programmed. Suppose we were to begin making artificial organisms to act as slave labor—androids. What kind of minds would we give them? What kind of abilities and behavioral traits? Wouldn't we turn out something like the Sets? They're perfect slaves—as is obvious from the way that the colony here has made use of them. It's the one answer that fits the problem like a glove. The Sets have been such a boon to the colony because that's what they were intended *for*.

"There aren't two naturally occurring species of coding molecule here—there's only one. The other one was imported. It was imported to these mountains, and spread out from here just like the Sets. Geb was a colony world before we humans came here. The question is: how long before?"

"*And* what happened to the original colonists?" she reminded me.

"That too," I agreed.

"But how did they fail?" she asked. "Sure, there are human colonies which have failed, but in the picture you paint the whole point of having the Sets is to cut down the risk. *Our* colony didn't fail, with the Sets to help it. If the accounts of the witnesses are to be trusted it's succeeded beyond our wildest dreams—certainly beyond the aspirations of any other human colony."

"Think about it," I said—cheating a little, because I'd been trying to paper over that particular crack in the wall for the last couple of hours. "Because their capabilities are so much greater, their strategy would be different too. We send out a minimal colony, whole and entire. We send out thousands of people and the essential working core of a civilization . . . a human world in embryo, expected to grow over a few hundred years to some kind of maturity. It's a hazardous business and a costly one—costly in terms of the burden that's placed on the people who go out as pioneers. But if we had androids, we wouldn't have to do it that way. We wouldn't send out a colony consisting of a world in embryo. We'd send out a vast army of androids, with just enough people to supervise them in their labor. Maybe a hundred men would be enough—

maybe forty or fifty, if they were particularly adept at their job. It's only their genetic engineering technology that has the advantage of the extra breakthrough—they can't send more ships or be forever hopping back and forth from colony to colony or even from the homeworld to the colonies. But they do the job in two stages—Sets first, colonists later.

"Here, something went wrong. There was an accident. The supervisors needn't have been killed—if they were only an advance guard they probably didn't constitute any kind of breeding unit. There may have been an explosion at their base—that crater needn't be volcanic at all, and Gley obviously nurtures some suspicion that it was caused by a nuclear explosion, hence the radiation-measuring equipment. Maybe the second stage was aborted and the world was written off . . . possibly because it's a long way from the aliens' homeworld. That's a lot of ifs, I know, but if some of them are wrong there are others in reserve."

"You haven't got an atom of proof," she observed. Her voice was still level and her tone neutral. I couldn't tell what she thought of the idea.

"Of course not," I replied. "If I had, do you think I'd be contemplating anything as stupid as a descent into those fissures. But don't you see that it's necessary to check this out, even if the probability is low . . . because if it *is* true . . . ?"

"If Gley's working on the same hypothesis," she said, "it explains why he's so interested in the possibility of dating whatever happened in the crater. But it must have been a *long* time ago. The Sets spread out over two continents . . . the plant and animal species working their way all the way round the world . . . that must have taken thousands of years."

"I don't know," I said. "I wish I could be sure. Maybe it did take thousands of years. Or millions. But there's no way of knowing what kind of seeding program the alien project involved. Suppose the crater *was* once hot and has now cooled down . . . that suggests a long timespan as well. But we need something that will give us more than a vague guess—something quantitative. Maybe we can get that from the crater's soil."

"If it *wasn't* thousands of years ago . . ." she began.

I interrupted her quickly to stop her stealing my punch-line. ". . . they may be back," I confirmed. "If it was only five hundred years, for instance."

"But there's nearly a hundred and eighty years gone by since the survey team was here," she pointed out.

"We don't know what timescale these people operate on. If they're good enough at genetic engineering to make the Sets, what can they be capable of doing for themselves? Longevity might come easy . . . even immortality. And don't forget that it took *us* a hundred and fifty years to check up on our colony. If we'd found a disaster area how long would it have been before we tried again here? Another couple of centuries? Maybe never. And maybe *they* never came back, either. But we have to know when they *were* here, if only to be able to hazard a guess at where they might be now. And wherever they might be, *if* they're there at all, it means a great deal that they exist. Intelligent humanoids in our part of the galaxy, attempting to settle Earth-type worlds . . . that's big news. Big enough to change the UN's thinking on the space program. What price insularity and the one-worlders now?"

She let a few minutes drag by while she mulled over the whole issue in her mind.

"This isn't the colony farthest from Earth," she observed.

"No," I said, "but it is in this direction. So far as accurate surveys are concerned known space is a sphere extending out from the solar system with one or two little bulges on it. The world's that are farther away from Earth are at least fifty degrees away from this one. In this particular direction—and don't forget that we're practically at right angles to the line which leads from Sol to galactic center, where the main push is directed—there are only three solar systems farther out than this one that have even been surveyed. They're all useless. There could be Earthlike worlds within ten light years already colonized by the aliens. I'm not saying there are . . . just that there *could* be. We don't know . . . but we're going to have to find out. We *have* to—maybe even on the strength of the hypothesis."

She shook her head at that. "It's a pretty story," she said, "but that's all it is. Just a story. The UN isn't going to be persuaded to act on it unless you find some proof."

I shrugged. "I believe you. That's why I think it's important that we should leave no stone unturned. I think our best bet is to dig our way into the crater. But Gley wants to take the longer shot, and I think I'm with him, if it comes to the crunch."

"It means that much to you? To you, personally?"

"Yes it does."

"Why?"

"Because I think we need broader horizons. Not just in space but in possibility. We need to recognize that we aren't alone in the universe, and that it wasn't made for us. We need to cultivate a cosmic perspective."

"We?"

I colored slightly, and turned my attention to the donkey's reins for a moment.

"You can take it to mean what you want," I said. "The human race. People like me. You and I. Just me, if you like."

"You don't think it makes any difference?"

"I'm just as entitled to have an opinion about what the human race is and ought to be as the one-worlders are. I'm not claiming that my opinion is backed by God. It's just what I think is right."

"And you'll risk your neck for it?"

"Every time."

"And what about Gley? What's he in it for?"

"He's in it for much the same reason I am, leaving out the opinions regarding the future of the race. He's not so different from you or me. He wants to be sure that he's right. He's got an idea and he can't let go. He wants proof in order to satisfy his craving for justification. That's first and foremost. On top of that . . . well, he's instituted in his own mind some kind of competition between himself and the establishment, particularly Helene Levasseur. He wants to find proof before she and the law find some excuse for moving in on the action and taking it away from him. And over and above that it's a matter of some importance for the colony to know whether they ought to expect a visit some time in the future from an alien race whose property it's borrowed and whose abilities are far superior to its own. There are good enough reasons on the rational level, though I don't doubt that the ones which are driving him so hard are the personal and private ones."

"It would be bad enough," she said, "ending up a martyr to your own cause. But do you really want to be a martyr to *his*?"

"If he goes down," I said, "then I'll go down with him. That way, perhaps neither of us will end up martyred."

"Or both," she pointed out. She had always had a strong practical streak. She had a very down-to-earth outlook on life. She wasn't overtly cynical in the way that Karen was, but sometimes I suspected that beneath that calm exterior there beat a heart of pure granite. There would have to be, of course, if she really were the opposition's spy—the devil's advocate.

It was my turn to speak, but I passed.

"You could sit on top and wait," she pointed out. "*We*'re in no desperate hurry. We can dig into the crater from the top to find out whether there ever was an installation there to explode. We can take all year, if necessary."

"It's not our crater," I replied. "It's Gley's."

❧ 11 ❧

We found the dead Set on the animal trail that led toward the center of the crater, outside the pitfall trap. It was a pretty sickening sight. Whatever had done it hadn't been a great believer in waste; the flesh had been torn from the bones and the bones scattered. The head and one of the tibia/fibula sets were gone. A couple of carrion birds flew squawking from the remains as we approached, but they had not had the time to plunder the remains to any great extent. It appeared that they had not been left overmuch to plunder. There was blood all over the grass but there was very little in the way of evidence to indicate what kind of creature had been responsible. The ground was too hard to take tracks of any resolution, and the scuff-marks in the soil were anonymous—they could have been caused by almost anything. There were the occasional imprints of claws, but these were just scratches—no weight had been leaning on them and they were presumably the marks of forepaws which had been busily working at the bones rather than supporting the bulk of the predator. I picked up some gnawed cartilages to look at the tooth marks, and was surprised to find the impressions of quite tiny needle-pointed teeth as well as the marks of grinding teeth.

"That's the sixth this summer," said Gley. "And three donkeys. "Year after year it gets worse. Either the thing gets greedier or there's more than one."

"To judge by the teeth," I murmured, "it's not actually all that big, Unless, of course, it has a great *many* teeth."

"It has to be big to strip a Set so quickly," Gley replied. "It's less than an hour since nightfall—this must have happened soon after dusk."

I shone the lantern around carefully, looking at the places where the grass had been temporarily flattened. "Either it changes its position a great deal or it has no great weight," I opined. "There's no grass here that's been crushed through having been sat on for any length of time by something heavy. And I can't see where it *came* from. There are plenty of marks just here, but nothing outside a circle a few meters across."

"Dropped out of the trees," said Gley. "My best guess is that it's some kind of giant snake and that those clawmarks are the mark of some vestigial forelimbs. Sometimes the body-impressions seem to be faintly scaled."

"In five summers you've never seen it?"

"No."

"Very discreet."

"Last year I tried keeping watch over a tethered goat, but it never showed. I scared myself half to death waiting, not knowing whether it might go for me rather than the goat. I might never have seen or heard it before it got me. I keep renewing the pitfall trap, but I don't hold out any hope for it any more. I only hope that if ever I do see it I can get in one blast of the shotgun before it gets me. The cartridges are big enough to blow a hole in a brick wall, and the shot scatters too."

"Just don't discharge that thing near me," I said. "I don't want to be the innocent bystander who gets mown down by accident."

He didn't seem overly impressed by this request, but went on toward the hut.

I glanced at Linda, and commented, "All this and earthquakes too."

"He's a determined man," she said.

"He takes it all very personally," I agreed, dryly. I couldn't really think very highly of him for the moment. I had a certain deep-seated prejudice against men who believe that the best answer to a problem is a shotgun that fires big cartridges and scatters the shot so as to preclude any possibility of missing.

Once we'd eaten we were taken by such a lethargy that there seemed no sense in setting up the apparatus that night—quite apart from the fact that it would entail clearing a space to work afnid the hideous mess of Gley's cabin. Like a true gentleman he abandoned the cabin to us and disappeared to the Sets' encampment. In the face of such generosity I felt obliged to match the gesture by letting Linda have the bedroom. Once again I found it very uncomfortable sleeping on the wooden floor, and the fact that this time I was stretched across the hearth next to the fire didn't improve matters any.

This time, however, Gley's impatience didn't allow him to sleep in. I was woken up when he came stamping into the cabin at what seemed to me to be an ungodly hour. I looked at my watch, but I still hadn't bothered to alter its mechanism, and it was still showing ship's time. I groaned a little, for form's sake, and went rummaging in my pack for some pills to resurrect me from my awful state.

Gley started building up the fire, then went out to fetch water for his kettle. Gradually, I began to feel better, and by the time I'd chewed my way through the dreadful mess that Gley thought of as a healthy breakfast I was almost enthusiastic about the prospect of experiments in impromptu dating.

We set up the apparatus with some difficulty, and took a few basic readings with a simple meter. There was very little background radiation in the crater's soil. If there had been a burst of radiation here it had cooled down to practically nothing by now. With much more sensitive apparatus we obtained a count on the amount of carbon-14 in fresh foliage. Plants build their cellulose out of atmospheric CO_2 and water and the proportion of radiocarbon in fresh plant material reflects the percentage of C-14 in the air.

Then we started looking for some very old wood. We went first to Gley's woodpile, from which he unearthed a great disc which was all that remained of the trunk of a particularly ancient tree.

"It was dead," he said. "I burned the rest. I saved this with the intention of looking at the rings under a powerful lens in the hope of finding something anomalous."

"And did you?" I asked.

"I couldn't see anything with the naked eye. Never did get the lens—not the sort of thing they keep at the farm."

We carried it inside and began to take flakes out of rings at varying depths. There were nearly two hundred and fifty rings. It didn't take us back far beyond the date of the survey, but it was a start. Carbon-14 decays into carbon-12. The carbon-14 count ought to decline along a neat curve as we investigated flakes from ever nearer the heart—that is, it should if the C-14 level in the atmosphere had remained stable over the two hundred and fifty years the tree had lived.

Four hours later we had a neat hand-drawn graph showing a neat curve exactly as expected. The C-14 level in the atmosphere had been exactly the same two hundred and fifty years ago as it was today.

"Well," said Linda, "that's the easy one out of the way. Now let's get on to finding out just what's in the soil and the various rocks."

That wasn't so easy. The general theory was the same but the actual task to hand was more difficult. First we had to identify the minerals in the rock, looking for traces of something radioactive—or traces of something that might well be the product of radioactive decay. Normally you can date rocks by means of estimating radiopotassium, but that particular yardstick is a little coarse. What we were hoping was that we'd find something in the soil that might be debris from a nuclear pile that had gone bang. We already knew that there wouldn't be much trace of the original fissionables left, but all we needed was a trace and a lot of breakdown product.

We looked at a lot of bits of rock—Gley had assembled quite a collection—but we found nothing. The rock seemed to have been formed long ago in the geological past, when the volcano last erupted. There were some pretty funny-looking specimens but when it came to analysis they turned out to be mere freaks of nature. He even had some petrified wood that he'd dug up somewhere, but that, too, was millions of years old, and had been quite unperturbed by anything that had happened in the crater over the last several million years.

I began to suspect that perhaps there was nothing to find.

"Look," I said. "You've dug at least ten feet into the surface, if only to excavate that bloody pitfall. Didn't you find *anything*?"

At this point I still hadn't bothered to tell him my hypothesis in all its gory detail in order to compare it with his own. We had been too busy, and his natural defensiveness didn't encourage a free exchange of ideas.

"The pit's in a natural crack in the rock," he said. "A cleft, maybe made by a quake with pressure from below. On either side of it the soil's only a couple of feet deep before it becomes unworkable—practically solid rock."

"How did you find the cleft?" I asked. "Happened upon it while you were digging holes in search of the remains, I presume?"

He looked at me long and hard. It was the fourth or fifth in a series of dark hints but he'd ignored all the others. Now that we were at a particularly low ebb, though, and were all feeling a little frustrated, he took more notice.

"Maybe," he said.

"If you're holding something back because of some deep-seated reluctance to let go of your last secret," I said, "forget it. If you've got anything else, let's have it now."

"How much have you guessed?" he asked.

I held up my fingers and ticked them off one by one. "Sets and androids. Two life-systems are competing, one having radiated out from here. The alien base here must have been destroyed. This is probably the relic of an explosion rather than a volcanic crater. You've been up here for five summers looking for the remains of what was here before it exploded. Is there more?"

He seemed resentful, but accepted the situation grudgingly. There was still a little gleam in his eye, though, and it turned out to be more than the reflection of the lamplight.

"You missed on one count," he said.

"What's that?"

"It wasn't an explosion—not the way you mean. There *was* an explosion, but it was caused by the crash. This is an impact crater. I think a spaceship crashed here—right on top of the base where it was supposed to land. Spaceships have a habit of crashing hereabouts."

I appreciated the irony in the last line, but I didn't really see that it mattered much, and I said so.

He shook his head.

"It matters. I don't know what they had on top here, but it wasn't much. It wasn't built of bricks. Maybe wood, maybe plastic . . . but something biodegradable. If they could make the Sets they wouldn't need heavy technology to build a base. These spooks are *biological* engineers. What they built was consumed—maybe fairly rapidly. It's not here to be found . . . because I'd have found it if I could. That's why nothing will show up on the aerial photographs. Since the base was established—and since it was destroyed—there've been wholesale changes in the environment here. Co-adaptation, as you call it, or complementary evolution, or what the hell. There's been no stable situation to be interfered with in such a way that the record of the interference would be preserved forever. There's nothing here at the surface or in the shallow soil. That's all gone.

"But you can't biologically engineer a starship. That had to be metal. And any mining they did had to be with heavy technology too. It's the underground ramifications of the installation that will have been preserved, where they cut their way into the rock itself.

"Now, if there was an explosion, it wouldn't be too difficult to get to that underground part of the installation— if there was *only* an explosion, that is. A lot of the force of an explosion goes upward, and most of the rest sideways. Even a nuclear explosion wouldn't have pulverized the underground part of the base. But the energy of an impact is straight downward. If a ship came down almost vertically, plummeting in free fall, there'd be one hell of a lot of energy to be dissipated and practically all of that would be absorbed by the mountain. *That* would smash up any elaborate series of cellars pretty extensively. Enough to leave no trace that anyone could recognize, even after a couple of hundred years, on the surface."

"But *down there*, driven into the rock to a depth we can only guess at, is the remains of the ship. That's what we have to look for, the only way we can."

"You don't have any evidence at all that your scenario took place," said Linda quietly. "You only want it to be that way so it will give you an explanation for your failure to find anything on top and an excuse to go on."

"It's the *only* explanation of my failure to find anything up here," replied Gley, aggressively.

"The alternative explanation," she said, "is that both you and Alex are wrong. Great minds may think alike, but they sometimes think the wrong thing. Consensus is no guarantee of correctness."

I felt that she was being a little overpedantic, but the failure to find any evidence of anything with the dating equipment was weighing a little on my self-confidence too.

"But it could be the way I see it," insisted Gley.

"It could be," she agreed. "But even if it is, what makes you think you can find something down below? Do you think fate owes you the favor—the miracle—of preserving for you a negotiable passage down to the wreck? If there *is* a little piece of fused metal down there that just *could* be the remains of a ship, where do you think it'll be? Encased in a jacket of re-fused magma is where—a jacket that could be hundreds of meters thick.

"Suppose you do go down. Suppose there's no limit to the fissures and the caves that they may or may not give access to. Suppose that there's an underworld down there. And suppose you can't locate your spaceship wreck, whether it's there or not. What are you going to do? Spend the next five years wandering about inside the mountain? Just when do you give up?"

"Not now," he answered. "It's too important."

"It's a fool's game," she said. "A wild goose chase. Even if you're right there could be no way of ever proving it. No way at all."

"All the rain that falls into the crater goes down those fissures," said Gley. "Some stays in the pools, but not so much. A little gets expelled as vapor, but very little. The rest must work its way out in a spring probably a hundred miles from here. A lot of water flows through the rock there, and it's worn away passages. I've been a little way into the fissures—I've seen them, though I daren't go down because of the gas. If there ever was an installation here, and there was *anything* left after the disaster, then the water will have carried it down into the deep caves. I don't have to find what's left of the ship. I only have to find *something*. An artifact of some kind. A metal tool. *Anything*. And to find it, I have to go down."

"It's a long shot that only a madman would play," she told him, laying it on the line.

"Then don't play," he said. "It's my crater, and my

game. Just give me the suit. You can stay up here and rot."

She glanced sideways, then, away from Gley and straight at me. I realized belatedly that the whole show had been for my benefit. She hadn't been talking to him at all. She'd been talking *at* me.

"Let's get something to eat," I said. "Then we can do a little more work. If we find nothing, we can sleep on it. There's always tomorrow."

The look she gave me suggested that she doubted even that.

12

That night, as I tried to go to sleep on the cold wooden floor, the doubts finally collected their scattered forces and began an organized attack.

If the Sets really were artificial organisms then why was it that their makers had left no trace behind? It was easy, of course, to invent an installation and then invent a spaceship to crash on top of it, scoring a hit so accurate that *everything* was obliterated. It was easy enough to wave an arm in the air like a conjuror producing a cockatoo and say that most of what they built was constructed out of local materials like wood and biodegradable plastics. But *any* theory you're determined to stick to in order to account for a set of facts can be extended infinitely by secondary elaboration to protect it against any conceivable objection. Once you're determined to construct a particular type of narrative all you have to do is keep twisting the storyline to fit in any awkward point that occurs to you.

Objection: if there *were* Set-building aliens, why on Geb would they establish a base here, in the middle of the most useless land on the continent?

Secondary elaboration: they came from a world where the atmospheric pressure was a good deal lower than sea-level pressure on Geb. This was the place they felt initially most comfortable.

That was easy. It was also plausible, in its fashion. If there really had been aliens, and they really had established their base here for preference, it was the obvious answer. But it added one more twist to the story, one more weak spot that was papered over instead of being filled in.

I realized all too well that if I were committed to another point of view I could probably build up a story just as comprehensive that made no mention at all of aliens. Maybe I could work something up from the notion of Sets as a decadent species. Maybe I could work out some new evolutionary subtlety to show up yet more of the weird and wondrous ways of natural selection. I'd discarded such accounts because of holes in them that I wasn't prepared to paper over, but in the cold light of objectivity—or in a savage crossfire of opposed commitments—could my hypothesis hold up any better?

I had one solid piece of evidence that I still might collect—if, as I'd predicted, the Sets did have a different variety of coding molecules, then that was another halfpoint in my favor. It was only half a point because coding-molecule variants *do* occur naturally, though not usually at the metazoan level. But even if it weren't so, and the variety of coding molecule was identical with the species characteristic of the other metazoan species within the system, it wouldn't prove that I was wrong. I could get round it by proposing that the Sets had been engineered out of some domestic animal instead of being built from the egg up. As evidence, the investigation might be slightly indicative, but as a crucial test it was useless.

The main problem was, I decided, that there could be no conceivable piece of hard evidence that would prove me right. How could I turn up a datum that would show conclusively that there never had been any aliens? What would such a datum look like? Any actual substance we found had to support the theory. If we found an artifact, or radioactive material that had leaked from a nuclear pile, or a brick wall or plastic zip-fastener . . . anything of that order could be conclusive. But in view of the fact that all the hard evidence that might exist supported my case, I had to accept the corollary that the *failure* to find any such evidence must be taken as cause to abandon it. I could, if I wished, cling to the notion forever, with the desperate tenacity of obsession, and no one could ever put up evidence to demonstrate that I was wrong. But that would make the whole story into an article of faith and not a scientific hypothesis at all. If I wanted to maintain my commitment, then I had to find something solid to rest it on; and I had to give myself a time limit of some kind. I had to specify what constituted doing my utmost to find the proof, and if—when I had done it—no proof had turned up, I had to be prepared to abandon the hypothesis, even if it meant letting the paradox of the Sets lie forever unresolved.

All of that had to be thought out piece by piece, laid out within my mind in correct order. It had to be, because it was my only justification for going down into the cracks in the northern crater wall, to follow the tunnels eroded by the water that descended from there into the bowels of the mountain.

For whatever reason, there was no evidence above ground. That much was clear. We'd examined the vegetation and the rocks, and found nothing we could confidently label anomalous. Gley had searched the area over and over in five summers. If there *was* something solid, then it had to be underground, no matter how or why it got there. And it *might* be quite a long way underground. Starting at the surface and digging down we could get down a few feet—no more. In the cracks that ran deep into the mountain we could follow the water—not to its ultimate destination but perhaps to some set of filters which would not only impede our progress but would stop much of what was washed down into the cracks by the torrents of rain. If there was nothing there, then in all likelihood there was nothing we ever *could* find, and we would have to accept our ignorance, or our wrongness.

Linda wouldn't come, I knew, and I didn't really relish the thought of being down there with Gley, who was already close to obsession, but I knew that I had to go. All this, if you like, is only rationalization—to excuse an insane act by dressing it up to look sane—but I was acting under compulsion. This issue was too important to allow any chickening out. Important to whom? Maybe only to me. But to me, it was all-important. If, somewhere out in the darkness, among the lonelier stars some distance away from the tattered starlight banner of the milky way, mere weeks away from Earth *via* hyperspace, there were people . . . then I wanted to *know* about them. I craved that knowledge—that *certainty*, if it was indeed certain—more than anything else. More than money. More than love. More than power—unless knowledge itself is reckoned as a kind of power, even when it is knowing *that* rather than knowing *how*.

I was quite prepared to risk suicide if, in exchange for the risk, I had a precious chance at that particular knowledge—the prize of prizes.

Every man, they say, has his price.

Sometimes, without for a moment admitting that I'm a cynic, I believe them.

13

The northern wall of the crater was a good deal more ragged than the southern wall. The one which I'd already crossed three times had been an imposing barrier with a steep drop on each side, but this one had a much steeper drop within and hardly any drop at all without. The slopes of the mountain bulked large above the rim, and channels in the rock cut right through the ramparts to continue into the crater—and into the mighty fissures themselves.

When it rained in these mountains it could rain very hard indeed—several inches falling in a day. Such rain would flood the caverns below with a torrent they could hardly contain, scouring their walls. But that happened very rarely. Most of the water that followed these channels came in a flood of gentler proportions that lasted more than a fortnight. It happened year after year at just about the same time, when the mountain that looked above us shed much of the snow that had accumulated there during the winter in the spring thaw. Because this side of the mountain faced north it shed perhaps a little less of its snow than the southern face, but we weren't so far away from the equator, and the sun was to the south of us in the summer noonday. The peak still wore a cloak of white, but it was the thin cloak that it never shed at all, not the thick, bulky coat it would wear in the dead of winter.

Because the inner face of the crater wall was nearly vertical here the cracks seemed like arches rather than fissures. They extended some way out into the crater floor before splitting into minor furrows, but in the horizontal plane they were shallow. The black maw of each tunnel-mouth was caught in the angle between wall and floor, and though their descent was in most cases precipitous they did indeed look like tunnels into the heart of the mountain rather than like bottomless pits aimed at the center of the earth.

There were a few stray wisps of water vapor belching irregularly from thinner cracks. I tested the vapor with my hand before putting on the sterile suit, and found it pleasantly warm—it cooled far too rapidly to scald. These vents were in the crater floor, farther in than the large holes, which exuded only an invisible miasma of foul-smelling gas. Much of the gas was the product of de-cayed vegetation which was swept into the holes by the various floods, but it was augmented by sulphurous gases originating *very* deep within the crust—the product of the heated rocks which remained from the era of volcanic ac-tivity, and which still caused earth tremors—though only little ones—about twice a week. The presence of the sul-phur—and, indeed, the heated water vapor—suggested that the cave system was extremely extensive, and no doubt elaborate too. There was no guarantee that people the size of Gley and myself were going to be able to get into a tenth of its forgotten corners, but there seemed to be reason enough to suppose that there would be enough of an underworld to permit an extensive search.

"Arne Saknussem would have loved this," I muttered, as Linda helped me on with my suit. She didn't answer, but moved away to help Gley with his. She was radiating silent disapproval.

"If the going gets too sticky," I said to Gley, "we're go-ing to have to be careful. Minor tears in the suit won't matter much—it's not maintaining sterile conditions we're determined on—but if it gets too hot down there we could slowly roast. There's no cooling system to speak of . . . the theory goes that the water-recycling apparatus helps get rid of some body heat and more can get through the filters as we expel air from our lungs.

"There'll be plenty of cold regions down there as well

as warm ones," Gley promised. "We'll not cook inside our skins."

We attached oxy-bottles just in case they should be needed in a hurry, but for the time being we were prepared to rely on the filtration system in the front of the helmet. Only if it failed to cope with the gas would we seal it and switch to the oxygen supply. We roped ourselves together and checked the security of the tools slung in our belts—pitons, crampons and things like small pickaxes. I had to admit that Gley had taken the trouble to equip himself well for life in the mountains. We had light packs containing a first-aid kit, spare fuel cells for the lamp and flashlights, and plastic bags and bottles for specimens. Gley had borrowed the crude radiation meter from Linda—a measure I approved of—but he had also decided to carry his shotgun—a measure I decidedly didn't approve of. He had the gun slung across his shoulder on a leather strap, and it seemed to hang comfortably enough, but I couldn't help feeling that it was likely to be an unwelcome encumbrance in any particularly tight spot.

Anyone can be wrong.

We walked into the mouth of the fissure that Gley had previously selected (on what basis I don't know) as the best bet. It wasn't the biggest, but it did have a channel extending into the crater as well as out, thus draining water from both the mountain and the crater. As we passed into the gloom I couldn't help thinking that some graffiti artist ought to have decorated the entrance with the motto from Dante's Inferno or something equally suitable. I looked back, in defiance of Orphean tradition, and waved to Linda. She gave me a token salute, and then turned around to walk back to the cabin.

"Ah well," I said to Gley, "at least there's a chance you'll get your washing done. Not much else to do while she's waiting except talk to the ship on the radio."

He just grunted in reply.

As the tunnel narrowed and plunged downward we had

to go in single file, and there was no prospect of conversation. The "floor" of the tunnel sloped at about thirty degrees from the vertical, on average, but was more or less smooth. This created difficulties by making handholds and footholds scarce and uncertain. As we went deeper, the tunnel became thinner and deeper. There was no problem at all with the height, but occasionally we had to squeeze through between walls that were barely far enough apart to let us pass. It was a tricky operation, necessitating the removal of the packs from our shoulders and a certain amount of scraping that didn't do the suits any good at all. Luckily, though, the walls had been pretty well scoured by the water of past rainy seasons and there were very few awkward spurs and ridges.

Despite the frequent interruptions caused by difficult passages our progress was good during the first couple of hours. Gley led with steady determination, getting on with the job but taking no risks. Whenever he was in doubt he let the flashlight down on the end of one of the ropes so that he could judge the steepness of the descent and map out the footholds. I slipped a couple of times, and on one occasion I slid right down on top of him, but he was as steady as a rock—I gained a lot of confidence just knowing he was there to catch me. He'd done a lot of mountaineering in recent years, and to him the descent was child's play. There was no steam here, and the air was quite still as far as I could judge. The filters took care of the pollutant gases without any trouble.

Gradually, as time went on, the slope got a little steeper, until it was only fifteen degrees or so from the vertical. That's precipitous enough by any standards, and it slowed us down appreciably. I became almost grateful for the narrowness of the slit, for it was always possible to extend my arms to either side and brace myself, and I could search for footholds to either side as well as in front of me. Gley would guide my feet whenever I got into difficulty. I got the feeling that this not only reassured me but also reassured him—he needed to feel that he was in charge and that this was his show. I wasn't about to argue with him. Any discovery we made could go down in his name for all eternity so far as I was concerned.

I lost track of time, and there was no way that I could estimate how far down we had come. My arms began to ache and I began to hope fervently that we'd reach some kind of bottom soon. I wanted a cave, or a ledge, or anything that would give us a chance to rest. I also felt hot and sticky, though the temperature outside must have been close to freezing-point. The suit's thermal insulation was a fraction better than its water-recycling ability and it needed a sweatless interval to catch up. Mercifully, though, the rock faces that surrounded us never became vertical or altered their inclination to the point at which passage would become extremely dangerous.

We stopped after about two and a half hours while Gley let the light down for the fifth or sixth time.

"It's okay," he said, his voice muffled and sounding rather as if he had a heavy cold. "We ran out of hill and we'll have to let ourselves down on the rope. But the drop's only twelve feet or so onto a stone floor."

"Are your sure?" I asked, knowing that it was a silly question but wanting so much to *be* sure.

"I'm going to hammer a piton into the rock," he said. "There's a crevice here. Then I'll double up the rope and let myself down. You follow. We'll leave a length of the rope here so we can get back up."

I braced myself, and waited for him to complete the task. It was routine, and it didn't take long, but the wait was doubly painful because I knew that when it ended I could relax for a bit and recuperate.

Eventually, he said: "I'm on the rope." And, a few minutes later, "I'm down."

I eased myself down to the piton, then locked my legs around the rope. I let myself down a foot at a time, feeling a sudden, irrational need to be doubly careful. I didn't look down until my feet actually touched bottom.

Gley had moved away from the rope a little and his body was shielding his flashlight. I looked past his silhouette to see what he was looking at.

The beam of the torch was reflected back from walls which glittered with crystals of one kind or another, and also from something dead white. They were bones.

Gley knelt to look at them as I came to his shoulder. They were scattered on the floor, caught by ridges that followed contour-lines around a shallow bowl whose center was beneath the tunnel-mouth from which we'd descended. There were thin cracks extending out from the center into which a certain amount of water could seep, but when the water was really flooding down from above, the bowl obviously filled up. I didn't look around immediately for the overflow—I was more interested in the debris.

There weren't all that many bones—they just showed up well against a matrix of stone and vegetable debris. They were mostly tiny—the remains of creatures no bigger than a rat—but some were much larger. They were limb bones from Sets or goatlike animals. There was one skull that had once belonged to a Set.

"These didn't get carried down here by the rain," said Gley ominously. "The small ones, maybe . . . but not this."

This was the skull of the Set. It had been picked clean of every last vestige of flesh but it wasn't very old.

"Maybe your predator uses the fissures as natural trashcans," I suggested.

"And maybe this is where it hides out when it's daylight up above," he replied.

"Breathing sulphur dioxide?"

"There's not that much poison in the air. Enough to make it dangerous for *us*—but a creature that built up a certain tolerance could take it. And the methane too."

"It would have to hate the light quite a lot," I said.

"Adaptation to living in volcanic caves doesn't sound like a very safe evolutionary policy to me."

"This range has been extinct for thousands of years," he said.

Obviously he found a certain aesthetic compulsion in the conviction that the solution to *all* his mysteries lurked down here. I was only half-prepared to accept the suggestion. I shone my own light around more widely, trying to tell myself that I was just interested in the lay of the land rather than checking that the predator wasn't sat on it's haunches licking its lips while it watched us from some handy covert. The cave seemed to be approximately globular—like a great bubble in the solid rock. Its walls were vertically ridged, though the ridges had been smoothed out to a series of folds like the folds in a curtain. There were two main exits, both slightly below the "equator" of the bubble. Either looked capable of taking our bulk. There were also smaller vertical cracks between the folds. There was nothing of any size lurking close at hand, though the glare of the torch picked out a number of small invertebrates—worms and arthropods—all very pale in color. With a constant supply of fresh water and fresh vegetable debris from above there was a thriving little community here, though the largest predators revealed by the flashlight beam were things that looked remarkably reminiscent of harvest spiders.

Gley was sorting through the bones carefully, turning the larger ones over in his hands.

"They're marked," he said. "The same kind of teeth."

It wasn't a surprise. I shrugged.

He picked up the skull and stared at its blank eye sockets. He refrained from quoting Shakespeare, though I had a pretty good idea he might have known the Set well and might even have called him Yorick.

"If there are more of these bones," he said, "some might go back a long way. A very long way."

"They might," I agreed. "But the water will have carried them all the way down. And bones rot. Especially in dilute sulphuric acid. The water coursing through here is fresh enough . . . but right down below, where anything carried by the floods reaches a permanent resting place . . . bones don't survive forever unless they're dry, or become embedded in sedimentary rocks. Don't build up your hopes too much on that score. And that's without taking into account the other obvious objection."

"What's that?" he asked.

I was surprised he hadn't worked it out years ago, but it seemed that his thoughts had never before turned to the possibility of there being actual skeletal remains.

"If you could design androids," I said, "what would they look like?"

"Oh," he said, seeing the thrust of the argument. If the Sets looked like the Set-builders—which they very well might—how would we know if we found the skull of an alien?

"Even if we did find a skull that looked a little different," I said, "we wouldn't have proof. It could always be argued that it was an aberrant Set . . . or even a member of a slightly different species which now no longer exists. We need more than bones. We need artifacts."

Gley dropped the skull, regretfully.

The silence seemed particularly profound once the echo had died away, and I strained my ears trying to catch a sound that wasn't there. I found a place to sit where I could lean back against the wall and I reached into the pack for a couple of tubes of broth. I warmed them up by the heat of the larger lamp. While I was doing that Gley went to shine his flashlight into the two afferent tunnels.

"We'll take this one," he said, on due consideration, indicating the one which was most nearly opposite to the direction of slope of the tunnel we'd descended. To judge by the grooves in the rock, that was the one that took more of the water out of the cave. It was also the one which pointed at the heart of the mountain.

When we'd rested for the best part of an hour, I felt fit enough to go on. By that time Gley was already a little bit impatient.

This time it was a little easier in that the slant of the tunnel was more gentle. But the tunnel was more nearly circular in section, and this meant that we were often reduced to crawling like worms. Getting through the narrow passages was like trying to force corks through bottlenecks.

We were no longer in a simple shaft—here the walls were frequently cracked and faulted, and the gas coming up through some of the cracks was warm. The walls were wet with a greasy dampness that gave me the uncomfortable feeling that the walls were suppurating. I didn't like the way that some of the stickiness came off on to my suit, lubricating it. I could keep the gauntlets and my helmet free of the stuff, but I worried about the boots and the footholds they might slip out of. Had the way been as steep as it had previously I would have wanted to call the whole thing off, but it was unpleasant rather than actually dangerous.

I kept glancing at my watch occasionally to note the passage of time since the resting place, but it was still registering ship-standard time, and though it didn't matter a damn down here how long the hours and minutes were by comparison to the planetary day I still had the feeling that the hour indicated was unreal and lacking in meaning.

Inevitably, I began to have second thoughts about the wisdom of all this. If there *had* been an underground installation it was obviously way above us by now. There had been no sign whatever of human or alien agency in the bubble-cave where we'd stopped. If there were signs that the crater area had once been inhabited in a lower cave-system then nothing significant had descended by the way we were coming. Except perhaps a mysterious predator—a monster from some mysterious underworld. We seemed to be miles below the surface now, though my watch assured me that was nonsense. It seemed like an age since I had last seen the light, but it was only a matter of hours, and though we seemed to have moved quickly we had been making our way in a painstaking fashion. It was easy here to fall prey to the illusion that we had entered another world remote from the one we had left, and that there could be no connection between this wet wormhole curling its way claustrophobically through the mountain and the world of trees and multicolored blossoms beneath the infinite sky, but illusion it was. We were still within the planet's outermost shell, nor could we ever hope to penetrate it.

Eventually, after nearly getting stuck and being forced back, we found another section that was almost level, where we could comfortably sit and rest. The tunnel had veered away to one side by now, and we were hardly getting deeper at all. The walls were uniform, almost polished. Their basic color was gray but they were streaked here and there with white and sometimes with green.

"This was never a blow-hole," observed Gley. "This rock's never been molten. The only thing that's ever come this way is water."

He asked me for the radiation meter, and he checked the rock. The little red numbers hardly changed at all as he held the sensor against the rock. Radioactivity was negligible—less than the background count up above. We checked the temperature for form's sake. It was 5°C. A little warmth in the rock but nothing special. Gley managed to find a little fluff in the bottom of his packsack, and he let it go in mid-air. There was no significant air current.

"Not very hopeful," I observed.

"The tunnel's leveling off," he said, absently. "There's probably another cave-system at this level. We certainly aren't down to the water table yet. The water comes down here—there must be some kind of sink that it goes *to*."

"Sure," I said, unenthusiastically. "Probably just around the next corner."

And, as luck would have it, I was right.

❀ 14 ❀

This time it was no mere bubble but a *real* underworld. It was a place where we could walk upright through chambers with vaulted ceilings on floors that were more or less level. There was no knowing how far the system extended, but there seemed to be caves and grottoes in great profusion. As we moved from one to another I had to keep scoring the rock with the point of a piton in order that we might find our way back. The shape of the chambers was irregular, and the ceilings especially were pitted and hollowed. There were crevasses in the floor which had to be avoided—most too narrow to fall down but nonetheless a cause of anxiety. From the lips of the cracks which ran across the ceilings hung stalactites—not in great profusion, but often impressive in their bulk. There were far fewer stalagmites, but here and there where water dripped perpetually a squat, rounded growth made its lazy way up toward its more graceful partner. I noted that several of the longer and thinner stalactites had shattered—sometimes the debris lay scattered below, more often it had been carried away by water into one or another of the abyssal cracks. Obviously the world down here was not untouched by the occasional earth tremors.

There were pools of water here, looking quite placid and lifeless. No light ever reached here, nor was there any significant warmth in the rocks. The only energy supply was the rotting debris carried down from above, and that was frugal. Most of it was washed into the pits—little enough became mud at the bottom of these pools. Even at the micro-organic level there was probably hardly any life at all in the water.

Some of the bigger pools, however, had rather more mud and offered rather more scope. The tunnel by which we had gained access to the system had come in almost horizontally, so that the torrents of water it occasionally carried would have gushed out over the floor to fill a dozen or more cracks, spreading its bounty thinly. But where any significant amount of water poured down from above it could eat out a bowl for itself which could grow deeper and deeper. There a thick silt might collect while only water carrying a light colloidal suspension of soil might flow out over the rim to disappear into the depths.

Where the rocks had not been worn smooth by water they were often covered with a sheen of lustrous crystals and pockmarked with small blisters, but whether this was due to the solidification of lava long ago or to the fact that the crystalline elements in the matrix resisted erosion to a greater extent I was unable to tell. Sometimes the bedrock formed spirals and fringes around particular spurs of harder mineral, but I was at a loss to explain how it had occurred.

We made much slower progress now, not because the way was difficult but because Gley was so intent on examining the surroundings. He dropped fragments of broken stalactite into some of the wider crevasses, and once or twice we heard them splash into water rather than rattling on rock. There was not much farther down to go. If we were to find anything it would have to be here. I had long ago lost my sense of direction, but Gley told me that in his opinion we were now working our way back from the direction of the mountain toward the rock vertically beneath the crater. Whether this was knowledge or optimism speaking I couldn't tell.

Periodically we checked the temperature of the air and took radiation counts. Soon we began to notice a change, albeit a slight one, as both began to rise very slowly. We were moving toward warmer rock, and perhaps getting closer to some subterranean source of radioactivity. We adjusted our direction to follow the guidance of the thermometer and the meter, and the hours slid past while we scored the rocks and gradually came into a slightly more hospitable region.

We came into a series of larger caves, whose walls were streaked with colors, often forming aesthetically pleasing abstracts which lured the eye to follow them in a hopeless search for pattern, shape or meaning. The crystals began to take on the aspect of galactic clusters of stars in my overactive imagination, and the blisters and pores became mysterious universal entities for which there were no names. My attention, I fear, wandered perpetually from the task of searching the cracks and crevices of the floor in case by some serendipitous miracle we should find a plastic ray gun or some other esoteric product of a long-lost surface civilization. My dereliction of duty was, however, compensated by the zeal of Gley's anxious gaze, which was everywhere in search of our own crazy version of Man Friday's footprint.

Then we came to the greatest chamber of all, and found what we had been looking for. I had not known, really, until we saw it, that it was what we had been looking for, but the logic was ready-formed in my head when I saw it. It was a pool of vast proportions—more than a hundred meters across. It must have been very deep in the middle. Around its rim I could see four or five places where water might flow out as it was filled up, but the important thing was that there was a steady stream of water running even now from a ring of stalactites set high in the roof of the cave. That ring of stalactites, I knew, surrounded a hole more than a meter across. At the moment there was only seepage running down its sides—but when it rained the trickle would turn to a flood. It would be like turning on a tap. And if the passage were connected to one of the other fissures that opened into the floor and the rampart of the crater . . . what might not have fallen into the mud in the belly of this pool in ages past?

I unslung my pack immediately. Gley was a little slower than I at realizing the significance of the pool, but when he realized I was not merely stopping for another rest he was quick to see the possibilities.

"If we'd thought," I said, "we could have brought fishing gear."

"I've got a crampon," he said, digging out from his pack something that looked like a small grappling-iron. "It won't pull out anything very small, but it might catch on something."

I was dubious. "I wouldn't bank on finding any old boots," I said. "Much better to wade out and fish up the mud in specimen bottles. We don't have to find anything large. Something microscopic will do."

"We could dredge up a lot of mud and find nothing," he pointed out.

"You could throw that thing in a thousand times and not even catch a pebble," I countered. "These suits are water-tight if we seal the filters in the helmet and attach oxygen bottles. They aren't much for swimming in but we can probably manage. The helmets are a bit buoyant, unfortunately."

Meanwhile, Gley had another thought. He began unloading his packsack.

"I can dredge up a sackful with this," he observed, unnecessarily.

It beat specimen bottles—especially when diving would be so difficult because of the helmets.

"Okay," I said. "Let me take it. I'll fish up some silt and dump in beside the pool. You can sift through it. Then we'll have more idea of what kind of wild goose chase we're on."

I sealed the filters and attached an oxygen bottle. The oxygen was released slowly, mixed with the air that was trapped in the helmet. As oxygen was leaked slowly into it, the carbon dioxide and the organic material I exhaled would be slowly taken out by the same filtration system that made sure the air sucked in from outside was breathable. It wasn't perfect but it worked well enough.

With the empty sack in hand I waded out carefully into the pool. The bottom sloped appreciably but wasn't ridged to any great extent. I trod on a pebble or two, but that merely reassured me that there was a lot of loose stuff trapped in the pool. When I was thigh-deep I bent over and submerged the sack. With some difficulty I managed to get it open reasonably near the floor of the pool, and then scraped it along. I could only feel an inch or so of sediment, but I did manage to scrape up a reasonable amount of it.

When I took it back to the edge Gley looked at it with some disdain. He had cleared an area of almost flat rock, and when I tipped out the contents of the sack most of the water ran off immediately, whereas I kept the mud from returning to the pool with my forearm.

"You'll have to do better than that," he said.

"I will," I assured him. "But let's not let our ambitions run too far ahead." I was already stirring the silt with my fingers. He brought the lamp up close and began to do likewise. Two fingers was just about enough to handle the job. The particles were finely divided indeed. There was nothing at all of any appreciable size.

Gley gave up in disgust after no more than a few seconds. He turned away and picked up the radiation meter. He brought the sensor close to the silt, and immediately the numbers began to change. They weren't exactly dancing, but they were doing more than they'd done before.

"It's radioactive," he observed, the excitement in his voice making it sound as if we were on the brink of a magnificent discovery.

"About as radioactive as the luminous paint on the hands of my watch," I mused. "Except that there's a lot more of the mud. A great deal more. It's not just the vegetable matter in the dust that's decaying."

"Something between here and the surface is radioactive," said Gley, his voice slightly unsteady. "The water leaches through, brings finely divided particles down."

I could see what he was thinking. The mysterious atomic pile embedded in the rock, inaccessible to everything but the seeping water, being carried away grain by grain. It might just be true—provided that the pile had decayed virtually to extinction. Even finely divided grains of uranium or plutonium should be a hell of a lot hotter than this was. But if there *had* been a pile, and it *had* cooled down, then there ought to be all kinds of things in the silt. All the breakdown products. And from a comparison of the density of the radioactive isotopes with the density of the breakdown products in the mud, one might be able to work back to an estimate of the time it had taken for the original materials to break down. In fact, with a little bit of sophisticated detective work using the apparatus Linda was guarding up in Gley's cabin it could well be possible. It wasn't much of a clue, but a clue it was. Provided we were prepared to assume that the original radioactive substance *had* come from a reactor rather than from natural ore. *If* it had.

"I'll try to get some mud from farther out," I said, turning back to the pool. I waded slowly out toward the middle of the pool again. This time I let the water come up to my chest before I stopped. I was now about twenty meters from the side of the pool. As I'd anticipated, I had difficulty ducking, and it wasn't easy operating in the darkness. Gley was holding up the lamp but that was a long way away now, and its light made no impression below the surface. However, I managed to crouch down long enough to get the sack down into the mud, which was quite a lot deeper here. As I moved it around, my arm brushed a couple of large, rounded stones, and then something else that was longer and thinner. I managed to get my fingers around it before standing upright again, but in so doing I let a little of the mud out of the sack.

What I'd grabbed was white, though somewhat slimed

with black and green. It was a bone—the lower half of the femur of a donkey. I carried it back along with the specimen of silt.

Again there was nothing in the mud that looked interesting to the naked eye. Gley loaded it carefully into a specimen bottle.

"How old's the bone?" he asked, after I'd reassured him that it couldn't possibly be part of a Set, let alone an alien.

"Can't tell," I told him. "But not very old. As I said, with sulphur dioxide dissolved in the water the pool's a weak acid-bath. In time it would soften the bone, and in the long run it'll eat it away altogether. This is still rigid. Probably not more than ten years old. Possibly a hundred. Not a thousand . . . but even if it were, what would it prove?"

"It proves that things which are quite large can get down here," he said. "So somewhere in there. . . ."

I took the point. I turned to go back for another shipment of mud. Then Gley let go a wordless exclamation. I thought he'd found something, but when I looked round he was bolt upright, listening.

"Did you hear that?" he asked.

"No."

"Stand still. Listen."

I stood perfectly still. The silence seemed infinite. But then there *was* something—first it was so slight that I was prepared to credit it to my imagination, but then it was repeated.

It was a scraping sound. At first I couldn't conjure up an idea to fit it, but I knew it had to be something scraping on stone. Something hard, I thought, but not metallic. Like the sound of a leathery boot . . . or a leathery foot.

Gley set down the lamp and lifted the flashlight, whose beam could reach further. He began to shine it around in a long, slow arc. I could see nothing, but I heard the sound again.

With his other hand, Gley reached for his gun—the massive shotgun that he had brought down because it made him feel safer to be carrying it. Right at that moment I was glad he had it.

"The thing doesn't like light," I said. "If this is its territory it's probably blind, or so nearly so that light is just a dazzling pain."

I wanted to add that logically it should stay away, but I wasn't so sure of that. If it was truly blind maybe the light wouldn't bother it much. And if this really was its territory then we, as invaders, were inviting attack.

The sound came again, louder now, and then again from somewhere else. Gley tried to catch it with the light, but there was nothing but shadows.

"It moves very fast," said Gley.

"No," I replied, feeling my heart sink a little further. "There are two. At least."

Then the light, darting quickly to the source of another sound, picked up a shadow that *fluttered*.

"Bats," I said. "It's not just one predator, it's a flock. Tiny teeth . . . clawmarks but no feet. It didn't have to be big to strip a Set that fast . . . just numerous."

It dawned on me suddenly that what had seemed like an enigma was no puzzle at all. We had been stupid to think of *one* organism when the analogy was there all the time. It isn't the big cats that strip carcasses to the bone in a matter of minutes back on Earth. The only creature which does that is a fish the size of a man's hand—the piranha, which has tiny little teeth and which hunts in shoals. The sound of leather on stone wasn't made by boots or feet . . . it was made by *wings*. Flying piranhas. . . .

I took one step back toward the side of the pool. Then I stopped, as the light caught more fluttering shadows. They were taking to the air. They moved as a group, quite soundless in flight. Even their echo-location noises were far too high-pitched for human ears to catch. For a few moments there wasn't much purpose in their fluttering, but now that they were airborne they were obviously not going to go back whence they came.

They *were* intimidated by the light . . . enough to be reluctant to attack. But they were also drawn here by an instinct that would almost certainly overwhelm that fear.

How, I wondered, had they sensed our presence? They couldn't see . . . surely there was nothing in the smell of our suits that suggested food. Maybe something in the packs . . . or the vibrations of our conversation. They must be inordinately sensitive to sound.

Gley brought up the rifle and fired. He was still clutching the flashlight in his left hand and he hadn't been able to aim properly. The recoil nearly jerked the gun out of his hands altogether. The deadly hail of pellets rattled off stalactites and outcrops of rock, and one of the fluttering shapes dropped from its flight, crippled if not dead.

Until then, they hadn't actually made a move to attack—they'd just fluttered around at a respectful difference. But now they went mad. The echoes of the shot were still resounding in my head when the black shapes arrowed in toward Gley. He was still trying to recover control of the gun, and he dropped the flashlight in order to do it. It hit the rock, bounced, and rolled into the pool.

He fired again, but this time it was a random shot and they were too close. Three of them thudded into his body, each striking at the torso. I could see now that they were each about a foot long, with a wingspan of two and a half times that. Their wings were leathery and batlike, but their bodies weren't furry. They were mammals, all right, but their bodies were scaled after the fashion of a pangolin. Their heads were reminiscent of the head of a snake, but instead of long poisonous fangs their jaws were filled with vicious tearing teeth.

"Get into the water!" I howled, knowing that Gley was finished unless he took action immediately. It was all the

warning I could give him, because the beasts were diving at me too. I put my hands up protectively and managed to fend one off. Another clung to my arm, but I took my own advice and flung myself full length in a desperate attempt to get as much of me underwater as I could.

I heard a gigantic splash which told me that Gley had either heard my yell or had stumbled over the edge of the pool in his desperate attempt to dislodge the monsters from his suit.

I tried to thrash about as much as possible, splashing the water up into the air. I didn't suppose that the beasts would particularly mind getting wet, but the spray would play hell with their echo-location and send them careering off in search of empty air.

I managed to get a grip on the one that was clinging to my arm, and tried to tear it off. The teeth were embedded in the plastic of the suit but hadn't yet dug into my flesh. I was rolling in the water in a horribly ungainly fashion, with the air-filled helmet obstinately refusing to sink but bobbing about on the surface like a stoppered bottle while the rest of me threshed the water. I clawed at the beast and managed to grab a wing. Its jaw wasn't strong enough to stay clamped as I ripped it away, and I could feel the wing-bones cracking under my clutch. I managed to thrust the creature away, sure that it couldn't fly or swim.

Gley was thrashing about much nearer to the edge of the pool, in no more than a foot and a half of water. There was so much water running off my helmet I had to feel my way to him, dog-paddling as best I could. I clutched his arm, trying to get him completely underwater, where the bat-things clinging to him could not survive. He was trying to wrench them off with his hands, but their teeth were caught in the coarse shirt he was wearing inside the suit, and they could not be dislodged even after I was certain they were dead.

Calmness returned very slowly as we both realized that the situation was getting no worse and that the air was no longer filled with fluttering shadows. Moving as if with a single mind the flock had fled, leaving at least five of their number for dead.

It took some time to prise the dead predators away from Gley's chest. The suit was badly perforated and the shirt was stained with a few tiny spots of blood, but no terrible damage had been done in the way of laceration. There was nothing that a shot of antibiotic wouldn't cure. There was plenty of tape in the first-aid kit which I could use to make temporary repairs in the suits. The repairs would hold up fine—in the air. The seal wouldn't be anywhere near so good if I continued to play about underwater.

Gley was cursing unsteadily as we made our way cautiously back onto the rock shelf. The first thing he did was reach for his gun.

"Steady!" I said, in a terse whisper. "That's what set them off."

He didn't answer. That was probably the most sensible thing he could do, if it really was the vibration of our speech that had attracted them in the first place.

I reached for the first-aid kit in my own pack, and muttered: "Pack up your stuff. We're getting out of here."

"No!" he said.

"We've got some mud. Maybe we can get a few grams more. But we're not hanging about."

While I spoke I was already taking tape off the reel to seal up my arm. He didn't make any move to start packing up, but inspected the rents in his suit. The little patches of blood were extending slowly.

"Just scratches," he said. "They won't come back. Not after this."

Even as he spoke there was a sound of scraping, and fluttering shadows moved.

"They're not going to go away," I told him. "The smell of blood's in the air. Predators that flock like that tend to be simple-minded . . . all controlled by similar signals of a very basic kind. It's a matter of instinct. They don't like the light, but it didn't stop them before and they'll come again as soon as any kind of stimulus reaches the trigger level." I spoke in the same whisper, with my helmet very close to his so that he could hear well enough. I was all too conscious that sound might be one of the things that could act as a trigger. Being damn near blind they could hardly locate their prey by sight. It had to be a matter of the sound they picked up with the same over-sensitive ears that monitored their echo-location systems. Sound or smell. Or both.

I gave Gley a shot of antibiotic—only a small one in the tissues around the cuts. He didn't even wince. Then I started to unreel more tape, wondering if I had enough to do a proper job, looping the stuff right around his chest. I decided to economize and tore off strips to cover up the holes.

"This stuff wasn't made for sticking to plastic," I said. "It'll do as a temporary repair—it's airtight. But it wouldn't be very clever to start testing in under water. And it might be as well to bear it in mind that you were damn lucky. We both were. Landing on your chest or your forearm all they can rip is the plastic sheath. But if they were to get under your arm or at your waist they'd be tearing into the recycling systems. That could mean *big* trouble. They might have adapted to breathing sulphurated air, but we haven't, and at my time of life I don't want to have to start learning."

I didn't like the way he kept looking around, still holding the shotgun as if he meant business. I had the feeling that I wasn't getting through to him.

"We get out," I whispered insistently. "Now. I don't care if there's a treasure chest full of alien doubloons in there. It's not worth dying for."

More fluttering shadows. They were out there, among the pillars of rock and the stalactites. Waiting. I tried to remember how far back it might be to the point at which we'd entered the cave system. Too far. If we ran, and they followed us. . . .

And it wasn't only them we had to fight. It was Gley's obsessions. The two self-imposed crusades which had fuelled his sense of purpose these last few years: to gain proof that aliens had brought the Sets to Geb, and to kill the monster that had stalked his entourage.

"How many of them are there?" he croaked. He was trying to keep his voice down, but his throat was dry.

"It doesn't matter," I muttered, fiercely. "Discharge that thing again and you're likely to drive them out of their tiny minds. Think how sensitive their hearing must be!"

He looked at the pool. Near to the edge the surface was glowing eerily. The flashlight that had fallen in was still alight beneath a couple of feet of water. The water showed up greenish-yellow, as if it were chlorinated.

"We have to find something," grated Gley's unsteady voice. "*Something.*"

"We already have," I tried to assure him, though I was by no means sure myself. "The mud it radioactive. If the analysis checks out. . . ."

"*If!*" he retorted, too loudly.

"There's any number of things we might find in it," I said, trying my damnedest to build a convincing argument. "Whatever was up above has been washed down into this pool. We won't find any large lumps of metal or plastic . . . but we don't have to. *Anything* that's in the mud that couldn't have got there naturally . . . a few molecules of artificial plastic . . . fine particles of some alloy. *Anything.*"

"It's not proof," he insisted. "And it won't tell us how long." His eyes were roaming the shadows, now, trying to find the scaly forms that cast the shadows. The worst of it was that he wasn't afraid. The good, healthy fear that should have been welling up within was damped right down, under the control of more powerful forces.

"Are you prepared to *die* for this crazy obsession?" I demanded. Now I was too loud, too."

"This is the one and only chance," he said. "You came with me. You were prepared to take the risks. You can't back out now."

"Damn right I can!" I said, taking care this time to hold the whisper.

"Then go. Leave me here. It's my blood that's on the air. I've got the gun. I can handle them."

He was wrong. Dead wrong, in a more than metaphorical sense. I was tempted . . . really tempted. But I was also scared. For all I hated that gun, I couldn't keep the feeling that it *was* protection, a kind of security. If we split up, wouldn't we be doubly vulnerable?

I didn't want to start running back through the cave on my own. I didn't want to *be* here on my own. But there was no way I was going to force Gley to do what *I* wanted. No way at all. It was one hell of a situation.

I took a few seconds out to curse my own utter stupidity in letting myself in for this. But it was too late now. It's no good being stupid and then regretting it—somehow you have to realize in advance how potentially stupid you are. It had never been one of my strong points.

He moved suddenly, coming ungracefully to his feet. He waded a couple of meters out into the water and picked out the flashlight. He aimed it at a shadow which stirred, and then moved it round in a slow arc. The beam finally settled on the one he'd managed to shoot. It was nothing but a mass of bloody pieces, as though it had exploded. The others hadn't come to take it—I couldn't be sure why not. Predators that hunt in packs are usually economical in the matter of tidying up their failures. This lot apparently didn't go in for cannibalism. That was a real shame. If we could only get away, leaving the smell of *this* blood to take the monsters off our track . . . but it seemed that their instincts were stacked in a less convenient manner.

Gley took up the rope that had tied us together while we'd made our long descent. He tied a loop in the end and then fixed a crampon to the knot, partly to serve as a grappling hook, partly as a weight. It was the most ungainly substitute for a fishing line I'd ever seen. But he started whirling it round his head preparatory to making a throw.

It was crazy—in fact, so patently crazy that I even forbore to point out the fact. He seemed quite composed as he hurled it out over the water—not mad, just very stubborn.

The splash it made seemed horribly loud.

He'd had to put down the gun to make the throw, but he picked it up again and looked round as the contraption settled to the bottom. The creatures didn't stir from their hiding places. He gave them a couple of minutes, then set the gun down again and began hauling his dredge slowly across the floor of the pool. He didn't look at me at all. I watched helplessly for a moment or two, then began cudgelling my brain in the hope of thinking of something to do that would bring a measure of sanity, no matter how small, back into the situation.

The only idea which occurred to me was that I might improvise something from the medical supplies that I could smear on the outside of my suit to act as a deterrent or a poison. It was not the greatest inspiration I'd ever had but I was under a lot of pressure at the time. It *might* have been a good idea had I still had the medical kit that had been provided for the *Daedalus* mission. But I didn't—that was lost somewhere beneath the ocean of Attica, along with so much else that was essential. All I had with me was a hastily improvised first-aid kit that could just about stave off the more banal forms of disaster.

I watched Gley bring the dredge up to the edge of the pool, and listened to him curse quietly as he realized that the unevenness of the bottom would make it virtually impossible for him to snag anything but pebbles. There wasn't even enough mud to shake off the rope.

"Gather up the stuff," he said. Hope rose within me but was quickly dashed. "We'll move round the pool," he added, "and try to find a better spot."

It was, at least, an experiment of sorts. I didn't really hold out much hope that the bat-things wouldn't follow us, but at least they had the option of letting us go in peace.

I managed to get most of the stuff back into Gley's filthy and wet packsack, and repacked my own. At least we were now ready to run if fate decreed that we must. But when we moved along the edge of the pool we were putting extra distance in between ourselves and the trail we had blazed in getting here.

It wasn't easy, at first, to tell whether the predators were going to keep us within easy reach. The shadows moved behind us, but we could not hear the beat of their wings and the shadows which changed were mere projections from which it was not always easy—or even possible—to judge the distance of the things which cast them. I was able to hope for five minutes or so that we were getting further away from our nemesis.

But the shadows kept fluttering at the limits of the lamplight's reach. They weren't letting us get away.

We came into an area where the roof was lower, the stalactites reaching down almost to the level of our heads. The ground here was flatter and strewn with broken rock, with lumpy globular stalagmites growing up around and among them. Gley paused, and passed the shotgun to me. I accepted it, ready enough to use it if the black silhouettes came at me. Gley waded out into the water, testing the bottom. It was still no good. He came back and we went on for another forty or fifty meters. He was looking at the pool; I was looking mostly up into the air, watching the signals fluttering across the colored rock faces. Only occasionally did I bother to look down. That's how it was that I didn't realize exactly where we were treading until something cracked beneath my feet.

I looked down.

It was—or had been—shaped exactly like a pebble. It had been about the size of a hen's egg, and internally it was remarkably similar. The shell had been perhaps a little softer and more elastic. Like the egg of a reptile, or a *very* primitive mammal. I remember correcting, mentally, the metaphor I'd drawn earlier. Not flying piranhas at all. Flying platypuses with piranha-like teeth. Quite a bizarre notion, when I really got down to thinking about it.

"Gley," I muttered hoarsely. "We're in the middle of their goddam breeding ground!"

❊ 15 ❊

I let the beam of the flashlight fall to illuminate the ground, and Gley let the lamp down a little. The first thing we saw was a cluster of white bones close to my right foot. Farther away we could see more bones . . . and more. I scanned the rock-strewn floor looking for more eggs, but couldn't see any. Then the light picked out a dark shape on the floor, just five or six paces in front of us. I'd passed over it twice, thinking it was a shadow, but now something about it made me pause.

Its wings were extended across the ground as it lay supine, its head held very low. Its head was directed toward us, and amid the tiny scales of compressed keratin I could see two tiny eyes, blinking rhythmically. Gley saw it, too, and took a step forward, dropping his makeshift dredge and reaching for the shotgun, which I was still holding. I didn't let go.

He turned to face me, looking impatient and rather angry.

I shook my head. Then I gestured back toward the darkness the way we had come. "If we start attacking them on the nest . . ." I murmured.

"You just trod on an egg," he pointed out.

"Either it was abandoned," I whispered, "or—more likely—you killed the one that laid it."

I was still pointing the flashlight at the one that was stretched on the ground a few meters away. I had no faith that it would stay there. The rocks here weren't particularly warm, but she could probably leave the egg for ten or fifteen minutes at a time without it getting dangerously cold.

139

"Those bones," said Gley, his thoughts now changing direction.

"Sure," I muttered. "Not just the produce of the season. Up high on the ledges, where the floodwater doesn't reach they could be pretty old." I didn't add: *And there just might be more than bones*. There was no point in adding my thought to his when his was more than enough to help us stay in trouble.

The flashlight didn't have enough range to find the wall of the cave at that point, though it did pick up a couple of steep steps away to the right. There didn't seem to be any bones lodged there, but the worst of the floods probably reached that high with ease during the big melt at the end of winter when the snows came off the mountain slopes.

"Give me the gun," said Gley, evenly.

"What do you intend doing?"

"I'm going to smash its head with the butt," he announced, calmly.

"And if they attack?"

"The more we kill on the ground the fewer we'll have to shoot out of the air."

"We can't fight them," I said, insistently. "There must be fifteen or twenty in the flock, and maybe half a dozen more warming eggs on the ground. It's too many."

I wasn't getting through. He *wanted* to fight. I realized that suddenly, with a start of surprise, and then felt a fool for not having seen it earlier. His finger was *itching* to start blazing away again. The first time they had come at him he hadn't been quite ready—or so he was telling himself now. *This* time he could get them. That was what he believed, as sincerely as it was possible to believe it. He was set on course, like a clockwork toy that was all wound up. Anything that got in his way was only going to hold him up while he whirred and buzzed and tried to force his way through.

I handed over the gun.

"Don't start smashing things with the butt," I advised

him calmly. "The thing will blow up in your face. If you want to use it as a club, unload it first."

He saw the wisdom of the advice. I could practically watch the thoughts ticking over in his mind. Gun in one hand, lamp in the other, rope-and-crampon on the floor. He weighed it all up. Then he put down the lamp and picked up the crampon, putting one shoulder through the loop of the rope and leaving himself just enough slack to swing the crampon.

"Bring the light," he said.

"No," I replied.

He didn't bother to get angry again.

"Then keep the beam steady," he said.

That I was prepared to do. I held the flashlight firmly, focused on the black shadow and the tiny blinking eyes. Gley moved out of the line of the beam, so as not to interrupt it. He took four quick steps, and then brought down one of the hooks of the crampon squarely on the monster's skull.

It didn't move an inch, but even as he struck there was another shadow hurtling past me out of the darkness behind. Where the one came, the others led.

Gley let go the crampon, whose point was still embedded in the head of the bat-thing, and brought up the gun. As I was practically dead in the line of fire I dived flat. I left the flashlight behind, dropping it without bothering to wonder where it would fall. The lamp was already on the floor.

The shotgun discharged once, then twice. There was no appreciable pause. I didn't want to know what the score was—I just got up on one knee in order to get sufficient leverage to take a long, flat dive into the water. I still had my pack on but there was no time for worrying about it now. In point of fact, the water wasn't really deep enough for it to get wet. I made a colossal splash as I belly-flopped into the water, but it was only a few inches deep.

I turned, crab-fashion, so as to face the place where it was all happening.

Gley was on one knee, the side of him that was toward me illuminated by the lamplight, the blue sheen of the sterile suit seeming to glow. There were cartridges on the ground—he'd spilled them from the box that he kept them in. The box must have been in one of the side pockets of the packsack where he could reach it in a hurry, but he'd been in too much of a hurry and fumbled it.

When I first looked there were no black shadows clinging to his body—just a flock of shadows whirling around him like some aerial maelstrom. There was no way I could guess how many he had felled with his first two shots. While he was still getting the gun reloaded one thudded into his pack, and then another. I saw him bend slightly before the impacts, but he didn't do anything to get the things off his back. Their claws sank into the material of the packsack, and that was probably all right by him.

When he stood erect again it was as though he had sprouted wings of his own—he looked like a hunchbacked giant trying desperately to take off . . . an early experiment in human flight.

He brought the gun up to his shoulder and sighted along the barrel, following the circling creatures as they fluttered around him. He fired once, and something was catapulted out of the maelstrom, crashing to the pebbled ground with a clatter. He fired again, and again he scored at least one hit. But killing your enemies two at a time is no big deal when you're using scattershot, and there were still far too many in the air.

Down on one knee again he went, but this time there was no chance to reload. The two on his back were moving, clawing themselves around to the vulnerable area beneath his arms, where they could wreak havoc with the circulation systems in his suit. And now there was a third which dived in—and got a grip on his helmet, right before his eyes. Everywhere else the suit clung so closely to his skin that the claws would go clean through into his clothing or his flesh, but the helmet left clearance. He reached up with one hand to rip the beast away, but found it too strong for him. He couldn't move it.

Realizing the danger of the ones on his back he threw himself flat and tried to roll, hoping to dislodge them. But they were tough enough to stand that. They flattened their wings across his suit as if they were giant moths hugging the trunk of a tree, and they clung *hard*. He had no chance of getting them off that way.

Now that he was down, the others no longer formed a circle as they whirled about him. They gathered above him, flapping grotesquely as they tried to hover. Two or three actually dropped to the ground, and moved in on him in a horribly ungainly fashion, thrusting forward with their wings as if they were using the tips to walk on.

There was no time left for innocent bystanders. He had made his play and it had failed. He was as good as dead unless someone went to help, and the only someone around was me. I could have rationalized it by the thought that after they'd finished with Gley I was next on the menu, but I didn't bother. I just hauled myself up and staggered out of the water. I ran toward him, already reaching out with my hand to pick up the crampon.

If their tiny minds had been able to contain more than one thought at a time they'd have heard me coming and sent a detachment to meet me, but they had a simple-minded hierarchy of instincts and they weren't exactly used to counterattacks. The whole flock was desperate to get their claws into Gley, and they didn't pay the least attention to me until I was on the scene and had the crampon in my hand.

Immediately I found problems. All the slack I had on the rope was the slack Gley had allowed himself. The rest was still looped around his body. I couldn't actually whirl the thing around my head like a battle-axe. I could get it up to shoulder height and then deliver a short, sharp thrust and that was all.

I hit out at the one that was on Gley's helmet, hoping to deal it some mortal injury without actually damaging Gley. I managed to hit it, but the point of the crampon wasn't sharp enough to tear into it. There was a flapping at my feet as one of the grounded beasts tried to get its teeth into my boot, but that was no trouble. I stamped once and forgot about that one. I hacked at one of the ones on Gley's back, but was still to half-hearted about it. I hit again, harder, hoping the pack would absorb the force of the blow. This time I must have hurt the creature, but it didn't let go. Once they had their claws in there was nothing that would make them let go except water.

It was a long way to the water, but Gley knew by now that he was beat and was ready enough to be hauled to his feet. I waved the crampon about as best I could, trying desperately to clear the air. I found, almost to my surprise, that one was on my pack now, climbing over the flap to get at the back of my head. Suddenly there was another at my shoulder, though I managed to strike that one with the crampon before it dug in deep. By now, though, there were four or five clinging to Gley, and they were reaching vulnerable spots. There were five or six still fluttering around us.

It was still a long way to the water.

Too far.

I tripped over a rock and fell forward, heavily. I lost my grip on Gley's arm, but not on the crampon. It might have been better if I *had* let go of the weapon, because as it was I fell on it, and although the prongs were slanted back one of them drove painfully into my shoulder just below the end of the collarbone. If I hadn't had the suit on it would have dug into my flesh and might have broken the bone, but the flexible plastic of the suit contained the point, and all I got was a terrible pain and the seed of a nasty bruise.

The fall didn't knock the wind out of me but it was by no means easy to rise. It seemed that the ground was shaking and shuddering beneath me, and that the tremor was communicated to my body so that every bone and fiber was vibrating, stopping me from coordinating my movements or even from moving at all.

The lamp was just ahead of me and as I looked up to see how far I was from the water I saw the lamp dancing on the rock, and then I realized that it wasn't an illusion. The ground really *was* shaking.

It was another mini-earthquake.

Only way down here it wasn't so weak and trivial.

❀ 16 ❀

For a few moments I thought I was dead for sure. Seconds before there had been half a dozen bat-things zooming overhead, ready to drop on me as I tried to rise, to bite their way into my back and my thighs, my shoulders and my head. But with the first vibrations they were gone, diving for the safety of the rock. They couldn't fly in air that was vibrating like the air in an organ pipe, and they couldn't use their echo-location equipment. The peril overhead was gone, and all we had to contend with were the ones that had already got their grip.

There was only one clinging to me—I'd managed to discourage the one that had settled on my shoulder and it had flown off with its friends. Even the one I *did* have to deal with was only dug into the packsack. I rolled on to my side, away from the crampon. The shaking of the ground was nauseating me, and filled me with a sensation like vertigo, as if at any moment the ground might disappear altogether and leave me to fall forever and ever. Had there not been such immediate danger to my person the quake would have terrified me half to death, but with things as they were I grit my teeth hard and took control just enough to release my right arm from the pack. Then it was only a matter of rolling free, bringing my left arm out with me. The pack and the predator stayed where they were and I rolled free.

I couldn't reach the lamp but I reached the flashlight. As a weapon it was no great shakes, but it was something. My feet were practically touching Gley—I'd been able to fall no farther away from him than the rope to which the crampon was attached had let me. He was on his side, curled up almost into a foetal position.

I brought the flashlight down like a club on to the beast that was clinging to his helmet. I was able to knock it off this time, and killed it with one more blow. The flashlight didn't go out, though its rim was badly dented. I couldn't hit at the others without hurting Gley. I started to wrench at them with my hands, and tore one away, crushing its wing bones in my fists. I didn't bother to kill it, but simply hurled it away. Where it had clung to the suit on the arm there was blood, but it wasn't much of a wound. In the meantime, though, the other three that were still on him had played merry hell with the suit's equipment, and they were still there. One had burrowed right into his armpit, another was at his waist. The third was ripping away with its teeth at the plastic protecting his groin. I went for that one first, clawing at his head. It bit through the plastic of my gauntlet and into my hand, sending daggers of pain up my arm. Somehow I got my hand around its head and wrenched backwards, trying to break its neck. It was too tough. I was so desperate by now I'd have bitten it to death if it hadn't been for my helmet, but now I got help from Gley, who started tearing at its wing with his own hand. Between the two of us we got it off and away.

The two that were left were the first two that had landed on him, and they were really dug in. Both had managed to create great rents in the suit with teeth and claws, and they were well into his flesh by now. Gley was moaning, and when I tore one away he screamed in agony. He was bleeding very badly from the wound that that particular one left behind. The pain left him helpless and he sagged back again to the rock floor, which was still shaking, though not so violently. I tried desperately to pull the last one off.

I grasped both the wings of the last predator, and got enough leverage with my right foot to thrust myself back-

wards. The thing came away, and again Gley screamed.
The monster twisted in my hands and tried to bite my
chest, but I simply hauled outward on both its wings,
stretching the delicate bones and breaking them. It writhed
in agony, and I hurled it away as far as I could.

Gley was curled up again now, bleeding copiously. He
was gasping desperately, and not simply with the pain. He
had been breathing with the aid of an oxy-bottle and the
system taking care of his air was ripped to shreds. I
fumbled at the filters in the lower part of his helmet,
trying to get them open so he could suck air in there.

But there was so little time to do *anything*, because the
earthquake was dying now.

The moment he was breathing again I threw myself
over him, crawling hand over hand to the place where
he'd made his stand. The gun was still there, and there
were cartridges scattered all over the rocks.

The ground was steady now, though the nausea went
on. I grabbed the gun and cursed the plastic sheath
around my fingers as I tried to pick up cartridges. It
seemed to take an eternity before I got the thing loaded
and snapped the barrel back into place. But when I
whirled, ready to fire from the hip, there was nothing
there.

For a moment, everything was still and silent. While
four seconds ticked by I was rigid in my position of read-
iness, my finger wound about the trigger, ready to fire but
with nothing to fire at. My mind seemed paralyzed, unable to think. For a time interval I couldn't estimate, I
had been moving on pure reflex, moving from one action
to the next without ever making a conscious choice. The
whole situation had *flowed* with a desperate pace. Now,
suddenly, there was nothing. The tremor was dead, but
the bat-things weren't yet ready for the final assault.

Four seconds gave me just long enough for the bile to
rise into my throat and for the fear to take a solid, ice-like
grip on my belly.

Then they came, shadows flapping into the circle of lamplight. No more than half a dozen—perhaps only five.

I let go the first barrel purely on reflex, and missed the lot. I don't know how the scattershot spread out without snatching a single one out of the air, but somehow it did. *That* struck at me like a knife. There was real, physical pain as the realization hit me that they were still there, still fluttering, and that the one last shot in the second barrel might be all I'd ever have time for.

If they'd come at me then, it would have been the end. If even two had managed to get a grip on me it would have killed my chances, second shot or no second shot. But they were betrayed by their instincts. They followed the scent of blood—all of them. They went for Gley, with an eagerness that had them getting in one another's way. Moved by the strength of a single, insistent, instinctive thought they all fluttered into the same confined space, each one looking to stall in the air directly above Gley's body, preparatory to dropping on to him and burying their snakelike snouts in his blood.

It was almost absurd, for their coordination was perfect, their timing absolute. For one single moment they were clustered together in a volume of space no bigger than a storage cupboard.

I brought the shotgun up to my shoulder, sighted, and fired. And this time the shot ripped right through them, blowing them away as if they were dead leaves caught in a breath of winter wind.

I swallowed hard, and the bile returned to my stomach. The stabbing pain eased, and was gone as if by magic. Even the cold fingers of fear down below seemed suddenly to relax their grip.

I found that I was shaking. It wasn't an earth-tremor . . . not this time.

I got slowly to my feet, and took two steps forward, then knelt beside Gley. The first thing I felt was a terrible wave of anger and disappointment, as I realized now that

I finally had the *time* to realize it that he wasn't going to make it. He was alive, but he was losing a lot of blood. Too much of his skin had been stripped away. His suit was in tatters, and already the poison gases were getting at his wounds. No amount of tape was going to patch him up well enough for me to get him back to the surface. He was going to die within the hour, and there wasn't a damn thing I could do about it.

I went to my own pack, intending to get the tape to patch up my own suit and a shot to kill Gley's pain and ease his departure. The last remaining predator flapped up into my face from where I'd left it, clinging to my packsack. It was a lousy takeoff—the beast was too heavy to haul itself up from a flat start without a lot more time to work on the problem. I stamped it down on the ground and brought my bootheel crashing down on its skull. I killed it with that one blow, but I stamped on it again, and then again, venting my frustration.

There seemed to be bloody bat corpses everywhere. A lot of the creatures were still alive, but helpless because their wings were torn and crushed. One or two could still move a little, but they were only jiggling up and down— they couldn't actually make headway. All in all, it was a thoroughly sickening sight. I deliberately shut it out of my mind while I gave Gley a heavy shot of pain-killer. He was still conscious, and he blinked at me when I slid the needle into his arm, but he couldn't get his mouth open because of a pain-rictus that had clamped his jaw.

I got the tape out, and sat down on a rock to seal up the few small punctures I'd contracted during the battle. It didn't take long.

Gley watched me do it. His gaze flicked down to try to indicate that I should tape up his gashes. I nodded, but signaled that first I had to clean out the wounds. There was no point in trying, from a medical point of view, but for the sake of putting up a show I thought I might as well do it.

While I was working at it the pain-killer worked its trick. The pain-rictus eased, and freed his jaw so that he could speak. His voice was a little weak.

"We got them all," he said.

"Every last one," I confirmed. "Unless there are more incubating their eggs. Even if one or two got away, the flock is finished. Maybe the whole species. There can't be many other environments on Geb like this one. I think they were some kind of freak . . . living down here, breathing foul air, with earthquakes twice a week and floods twice a year and volcanic eruptions maybe once a millennium in the good old days. Life is sure as hell tenacious."

The last sentence was an incautious one. *His* life was going to have to be tenacious if it was going to last even for an hour. But he didn't even notice, let alone care.

He tried to say something else, but got it garbled. He tried again, and I made out the word "stalagmite." His voice sounded sleepy now, his words were slurred as if he was intoxicated. The drug was doing more than kill pain. He tried to point, and I followed the direction his finger was trying to find with my eyes. There was a whole cluster of stumpy stalagmites, of the type that grow up where a drip from above falls on a group of pebbles and evaporates to leave its suspended salts to make an ever-thickening coat over the rock.

Only the seed of this particular stalagmite wasn't a pebble. It was something rounded, but it had two circular pits on either side of a narrow triangular projection.

It was a skull.

I got the dented flashlight and shone the beam on the curious mineral growth. I tried to guess from the amount of the deposit how long the skull had been there. I've no idea how fast stalagmites grow, but I knew that we were operating on a time scale that was a lot bigger than mere years, or even centuries. It was *old*, preserved against the ravages of decay by the sheath that had grown up around it. The lower part was lodged in a crack in the rock, but the whole cluster was resting on a convex shelf about a meter above the level of the cavern's floor. Gley had been able to see it only because he'd fallen in a rather peculiar position across another shelf, his head supported by a pillow of rock.

I got the crampon, and tried to hack the stalagmite free. It took four hefty blows, but eventually it cracked at its weakest point, both above and below the upper part of the skull. I was able to pick up the upper jaw and the cranial cavity, still encrusted with a lot of calcium salts and surprisingly heavy. The lower jaw stayed jammed in its crack, supported by the base of the stalagmite, while the tip of the upward-growing pillar rolled away.

I knelt down beside Gley again, and showed him the skull.

"If it's a Set," I whispered, "it's atypical. But there's one thing we can be damn sure of, and that's that the Sets have been here for a long, long time. If aliens really did come they came thousands of years ago. Maybe tens of thousands. They won't be coming back. Maybe they came back once, saw what had happened, and decided to leave Geb alone. One way or another, though, it was a long, long time ago."

"It's not a Set," he managed to say. He wanted it to be the skull of an alien. He wanted that *so* desperately.

I shook my head slowly, looking down at the top of the cranium and the sutures in the bone.

"I don't know," I said softly. "It's not quite the same . . . but it's so old. How could we know? How could we ever know? All we can prove is that *if* there were alien colonists they came here thousands of years back. No wonder they left so little sign up above. And that's why . . . if there ever was a burst of radiation . . . the crater's long since cooled down. It was always the likelier alternative. Ancient, not recent. But it *still* could be a Set. We still have nothing to show for once and for all, without any argument, that there was ever anything here but Sets."

As I spoke, I turned the thing over in my hand, weighing it speculatively. And then I looked more closely at what I saw.

And I realized that I *did* have proof. *I did* have something that spoke clearly and unequivocally about the presence here, thousands of years before, of intelligent aliens.

I was holding it in my hands.

❈ 17 ❈

I finally managed to struggle free from the suit and let it fall onto the cabin floor. Then I collapsed into Gley's one armchair. It wasn't very comfortable, but there was a good fire burning in the grate, and the smell of the cabin was better than the smell inside the helmet. For the time being, that was enough.

Linda put a cup of coffee into my hand, and I managed to clutch it instead of letting it slip through my fingers.

"You look terrible," she said.

"You should see the other guy," I retorted. Only it wasn't so funny once I remembered that there *was* another guy. *Had been* another guy.

"Gley?" she asked, having misinterpreted the remark.

"He isn't coming back," I told her. I was speaking tersely because I was still somewhat breathless. The coffee helped to pour a little life back into my body, but not much. I'd been down the hole a long time, and it had been a hard week altogether. Probably the hardest of my life. I'd covered an awful lot of ground, physically and imaginatively. All I wanted to do now was sleep for a week, even if I had to use Gley's filthy old bed.

Linda let me alone for a little while, but only so long as it was obvious that I wasn't capable of stringing more than five words together. She spent some of the time looking at the skull that I'd dumped on the table, but she didn't touch it—she just stared, and it stared back. If it was a contest the skull won easily.

"What happened?" she asked eventually.

"We ran into Gley's predator," I said. "There was a lot of it. I didn't ever get to count properly but I'd guess at

154

about twenty. They weren't very big but they were tough. They got Gley. I was lucky. I spent a lot of time under water and when I finally got out they lost flying time because of the tremor. You felt it?"

She nodded.

"I called the ship when you were getting the suit off," she said. "Just to tell them you were back. Helene Levasseur is on her way here—she reached the ship yesterday. When she heard you were underground, and why . . . she didn't want to waste time. She's camped out in the valley right now. You want to call again now?"

"Not much," I said, tiredly. "As long as they know I'm alive."

There was a pause. Then she said, "So Gley was wrong."

My eyebrows must have lifted somewhat. "What makes you say that?" I asked.

She nodded toward the skull. "That's pretty ancient."

"That only proves that it's a long time since our friends and neighbors came to call."

Now it was time for her eyebrows to lift a little. "I thought you'd brought it back because it was a fossil—to prove that the Sets evolved here."

"It's not a fossil," I said, "and it's not a Set."

She looked at me steadily. "Can you prove that?"

I said, "Yes," and I met her gaze steadily, just in case it was a competition. I wasn't in the same league as the skull, which had had several thousand years practice, but I had the courage of my convictions.

"Are you sure it's not just wishful thinking?" she asked, trying to sound concerned.

"You never liked the alien hypothesis, did you?" I asked. "Even while you were going along with it for the ride, you never believed it. You don't really want to believe it, do you?"

"Do you?" she countered, knowing full well that I did. She was just stalling.

"What have you got against it?" I asked.

"Apart from its being crazy?" Again, she was stone-walling.

"It isn't crazy," I assured her. "It might have been a pretty wild conjecture when I dreamed it up, but it still fit the facts. It still does. Some time between five and fifty thousand years ago aliens attempted to colonize Geb, but gave up because of some kind of accident. It shouldn't be too much trouble to find more proof now—it's just a matter of spadework. Helene Levasseur can get Gley's Sets to start tunneling into the mountain. When they run out of soil they can use pickaxes—or dynamite. Eventually, they'll find whatever's left of the installation. They have to . . . because it's there."

"Why is it so important to you?" she asked. "I don't see the reason for the intensity of feeling. Gley was obsessed—no one sane would have gone down that hole on such a crazy trip. But I don't see what's obsessing *you*, Alex, or why."

"It's simple enough," I told her. "It's just a matter of priorities. I came on this trip to prove that the colonies could work, as a means to the end of persuading the UN to reinstitute an active space program. The evidence we've got to support that case is a little shaky, even with Nathan's public relations work to bolster it. But no matter how strong the evidence was, the persuasion would still remain to be done. Even with everything we've accomplished so far, I couldn't be sure that the space program would get off the ground again . . . *really* get off the ground, with new ships being built, new exploration done and new colonies mounted. Now I don't have to worry any more. I've got proof that an alien race has sent starships as close to Earth as our starships have come away. The long time gap doesn't make a damn of difference. Somewhere farther out from Earth in this direction there's a world inhabited by sentient humanoids more advanced than we are. Maybe a whole host of worlds. If they were better at genetic engineering than we are fifty thousand years ago—or even five thousand years ago—think where they might be now. Think *what* they might be now.

"The universe isn't empty any more, Linda. We can't turn our backs on it now. No matter what kind of arguments any devil's advocate might throw up we have to set our sights on the stars again. There's no choice left."

"I see," she said, and I was pretty sure that she did.

"And it doesn't matter now," I added, "whether you're the devil's advocate or not."

"What made you think I was?" she asked, her voice steady and neutral.

"Nathan told me there had to be one," I said. "He claimed that the UN wouldn't have sent him out to compile a biased report without some kind of balancing factor. I hadn't really thought about it, but it makes a twisted kind of sense."

"Why me?"

"Elimination. Conrad's on my side, and he was with the first mission anyhow. Pete doesn't spend enough time away from his machines, and both he and Karen have a vested interest in starflight because it provides their jobs. Mariel's obviously out of the reckoning, and so is Nathan. That leaves you."

"If we wanted to play spy stories I could turn over practically every one of those arguments," she said.

I managed a weak shrug. "It doesn't matter any more," I said. "It's a dead issue."

"Did it ever occur to you that Nathan might be playing you for a sucker? Or even that you might be playing *yourself* for a sucker?"

I didn't like the way she said that. She sounded a little too confident.

"I'm used to that," I said. "*Everybody* plays me for a sucker. I'm an easy target. For instance, when you and I worked together in Latin America. I didn't know then that you were assigned by the UN to check me out for the

Daedalus mission. But you were, weren't you? Just as you're playing some kind of hand now. You're somebody's watchdog, aren't you?"

"If I were a cynic," she said, "and I were faced with all the crap you've just invented, do you know what I'd think?"

It was a pretty convoluted way of putting a silly question. I said, "No."

"If I were a cynic," she said, quietly, "I might be tempted to observe that in all likelihood you've completely mistaken the political background to this mission. It wouldn't be too surprising, in view of the fact that you were probably chosen for your lack of commitment to any ideal save that of getting the space program restarted, but one might expect that your fertile brain might at some time or other have thrown up a suspicion about the simple black-and-white terms in which you see that possibility.

"If I were a cynic, I'd probably suggest to you that Nathan has never told you more than half the truth, and sometimes less than that. Maybe he even tempted you a little because you seemed to swallow it so completely. He's a nice guy . . . very friendly, very concerned, very honest—on the surface. Underneath, he *is* a cynic, and he must know that the issues are more complex than he pretends. Maybe he's the only one aboard who does, because that's the way the bulk of the crew was selected. But Karen knows, I think, even if she doesn't know it quite well enough to voice it. And Conrad must surely suspect. The real fight isn't whether we start up the space program again, Alex, it's over who controls it. The real fight is about power. Power over the ships, power over the colonies. The colonies were worthless for a century or more while they were just little groups of people struggling to survive. Most of them are still that and still worthless . . . but some aren't. Do you think that in the eighty-odd years since the survey ships were recalled no one's given a

thought to starflight except idealists and dreamers? The
fight never ended . . . it just went into a phase where
nothing much was happening. Now it's livening up again.
Do you have any idea of the attractions of the notion of
interstellar empire? Do you have any idea what kind of
potential power there is in running and operating starships? It's not a great deal in terms of money—maybe it'll
be centuries yet before anyone stands to make any kind of
paper profits out of starflight—but that's not what counts
to the people with real power, Alex. They already have
all the money they need, and their pursuit is in search of
higher things. *Control* is the key. The battle has never
been whether there ought to be starships or not, except at
the street-corner level where the neo-Christians and the
other one-worlders peddle their social consciences. The
battle is about who runs the show, who *commands*.
There's been an eighty-year lay-off because there was a
deadlock—no one was prepared to pledge money without
a big share of the action, and for a while it was a matter
of 'if you won't play it my way you don't get to play with
my money.' But situations like that are always unstable in
the long term. The *context* changes, in this case because
all the while the colonies have been growing up. Things
will start to move again soon. They already have. You're
fighting for a cause that was never there to fight for, Alex
. . . and all the time you've missed the *real* struggle.

"Nathan's preparing a case for some faction within the
UN—the dominant faction. Pietrasante is their front man,
although who pulls the puppet strings is another question.
But the other factions will get to see the report too, and
make out their own case. Maybe they'll have their own
reports to give them a little bit extra to start, but that isn't
really important. The facts don't matter in the way you
think they do. If I were a cynic, I'd say that they matter
hardly at all."

She stopped abruptly, and the silence seemed thick
enough to cut. Then the fire spat at me as some sap

boiled and blasted its way out of the wood. I felt as if everyone were getting at me.

"And if you were a cynic," I said, laying on the sarcasm as thick as I could, "how would *you* read the importance of what we found out today?"

"If I were a cynic," she said, still keeping her voice light and low, "I'd say that the glories of the we-are-not-alone argument are so much Scotch mist. I'd say that what we found here—if you really *do* have more to go on than an almighty hunch—only adds to what we found on Arcadia. There are things out here which could be dangerous. If there *are* advanced aliens in this part of the galaxy it's going to help the case put by the military for *their* control of star travel. They'll call it defense, but what they call it doesn't really matter. The fact is that if what you say is true, on top of what was happening to the people in that crazy walled city, we'll have found what Kilner didn't—something that will throw a big scare into the people back home. And when the people are scared they turn to the military. Essentially, I'd say that what you've found on this mission will throw star travel into the hands of the hawks, because the doves will be disqualified. If I were a cynic, that is."

"You could be wrong."

"Anyone can be wrong," she agreed, calmly. There was just a touch of malice in her calmness. If the way that I'd imagined things were back in the corridors of power was simple-minded, then so was this. Her either/or was just as naive as mine, in its way. And yet there was an ugly edge to it. Our news, handled right or handled wrong, was going to frighten people back home. Particularly the news that there was a humanoid race, not too different in appearance from the Sets, practically knocking at our door . . . or which *had* been practically knocking at our door when the Egyptian civilization was just beginning to cultivate the Nile valley. The Sets weren't particularly ugly, but with the name to help them along they could be made to seem pretty fearsome.

The followers of Osiris had made Set out to be an evil god without too much difficulty.

And he was, in any case, the god of war.

"You don't go looking for a fight with a superior opponent," I said, hopefully.

"If that's a judgment on human nature," she said, "it's a very poor one."

"I think you're painting a distorted picture," I told her. "You're trying to put me down . . . but maybe you're trying a little too hard."

"You only think that," she said, "because you're not a cynic."

It was a low blow. I tried to grin and bear it. The subject seemed to be closed. No doubt my so-called fertile mind would mull it all over in time to come and probably get pretty depressed about it all. But for now it was easy to switch over to my own feelings about what we'd found, and my own estimation of its significance in human affairs. Somewhere out toward the darkness there was—or had been—a race of genetic engineers who had tried, as we were trying, to colonize other worlds. It was a long time ago, but that didn't mean they were dead and gone. It could mean any of a thousand things—and I wanted to think there was some chance that I might find out which. Not now, and not here . . . but maybe not so far in the future.

Someone had to go looking for the Set-makers, and all the way up from the bowels of the Earth I'd been creating a new ambition. I wanted it to be me.

I was looking deep into the ruddy flames of the fire, and for a few moments I lost myself entirely in my thoughts. The lids of my eyes drooped slowly, and my mind began to lose contact as I drifted away toward the fields of sleep.

"Alex!" Linda's voice cut across my wandering consciousness and brought me back with a jerk. I couldn't help feeling that it was a little unkind.

"What?" I asked.

"The skull," she said. "You haven't told me yet just how it constitutes proof. How do you know it's not a Set?"

I smiled, and even allowed the smile to slip into a little giggle.

"Oh, that!" I said, thinking it was my turn now to feel a little bit superior. "Turn it over and take a look at the back teeth. That's the best row of bonded polymer fillings I ever saw. Guaranteed non-biodegradable. When he was alive, he must have had one hell of a sweet tooth."

❀ 18 ❀

I slept late, despite the fact that the chair wasn't exactly designed for containing the comatose. I would have slept even later had it not been for the hammering on the door.

Being roused was bad enough, as there are few less pleasant feelings than being woken up into the same exhaustion that put you to sleep. What made it even worse was the peremptory tone of the knocking. It sounded positively aggressive.

I staggered to the door and opened it. Linda appeared in the doorway of the bedroom, but it was too late to save me the trip. I squinted into the bright morning sunlight. There were two men standing on the verandah, with a woman just behind them. There were several donkeys parked in the clearing and half a dozen Sets patiently waiting for the next command. One of the men waved a piece of paper at me.

"Johann Gley?" he asked.

I blinked and looked confused.

"That's not Gley," said the woman, coming forward to stand between her male companions. To me, she said, "You must be Alexis Alexander."

"True," I conceded. As it was perfectly obvious who she was I didn't feel it necessary to reply in kind.

"Where's Gley?" asked the man with the piece of paper.

"Why?" I countered, trying to read what was written on it while it bobbed up and down in front of me.

"We have a warrant for his arrest."

I coughed. My head was clearing by now, and I was able to digest the statement without too much trouble.

"He's not here right now," I said.

"Where is he?" asked Mme. Levasseur.

"Inside the volcano," I told her. "He went for a little walk into one of the fissures at the north end of the crater. I can lend you a plastic suit if you want to go after him. It'll keep the sulphur dioxide out . . . but watch out for flying piranhas."

To this little speech she could find no immediate reply. She stood staring at me, slightly slack-jawed. She was tall, her hair already gray although she probably wasn't more than forty-five. Her two companions were a good deal younger and they were each a couple of inches shorter. The one with the paper had lots of black hair and looked vaguely like a gorilla. The other was thinner and fair-haired. They weren't dressed like officers of the law, but that was presumably what they were.

Linda had joined me by now, and was looking over my shoulder. She didn't contribute any comment to correct the misleading information I'd handed out.

"You'd better come in," I said. "I'm sure Gley wouldn't mind my extending hospitality on his behalf. What's he charged with, incidentally?"

I moved aside to let them into the cabin. I watched their eyes as they entered and looked around. The expression of distaste on Helene Levasseur's face told me that most humans on Geb lived in slightly more salubrious conditions. They probably kept the kind of establishment that only people who've solved the servant problem can keep.

"Suspicion of murder," grunted the black-haired man.

"Who's he supposed to have murdered?" I inquired.

"A number of Sets. Every year he's come up here he's come back with fewer Sets than he took with him."

"Correct me if I'm wrong," I said, "but the story as he

gave it to me was that a human who mistreated Sets lost them—according to him they'd just fade away."

"Usually," admitted the man, giving the impression that he couldn't care less.

"It couldn't be just an excuse to trespass on his land, could it?" I asked. "Maybe something to give you just a little leverage in negotiation?"

No one answered that. Helene Levasseur had stopped wrinkling her nose and was looking at something on the table. The skull, as ever, stared back, imperturbable in its eyelessness.

"He wasn't murdered," I said. "His bones were picked clean by scavengers several thousand years ago."

The thin man had looked into the bedroom now and was satisfied that Gley wasn't hiding under the bed. He muttered something about checking the Set encampment and went out. The black-haired man waited for a glance from Mme. Levasseur, and then followed.

The woman picked up the skull, weighing it in her hand in the style made famous nearly a thousand years before by Prince Hamlet of Denmark. She didn't turn it over, and hence was unable to see the crucial evidence.

"It's not quite like the skull of contemporary Sets," she observed.

"Did you get your aerial photographs?" I asked.

She eyed me speculatively, wondering how much I knew.

"Gley told us the whole thing," I said. "Maybe a lot more than you've begun to suspect. The photographs won't tell you anything. Gley's combed the mountains for signs of something the aliens might have built. He didn't find anything. It's true that vegetation shadows show up on aerial shots where absolutely nothing's visible at ground level, but that only applies to land where the vegetation's stable. It's been too unstable here . . . various species in competition, various life-systems in competition, not to mention the violent weather. You helped us to crash for nothing. We nearly blew the entire *Daedalus* mission doing you a favor that turned out to be pointless."

She didn't bother to fake a guilt-stricken look, let alone apologize. She just stared poor Yorick in the face, contemplating the mortality of man and other creatures.

"Several thousand years?" she repeated.

"That patina on his skull is scale left by dripping water," I told her. "He had quite a stalagmite growing on his cranium. He'd been there for quite a while. You can stop worrying about visitors from outer space coming to have another crack at settling here. No one's going to claim your Sets or your world. Geb's been unclaimed for a hell of a lot longer than the legal limit, and I don't suppose it's going to be claimed now."

She adjusted to the news very quickly. She didn't need an hour to think it over. She was obviously a person with a very methodical mind. She put the skull back down on the table, refraining from asking the question which I had thought to be all-important. She didn't really care whether it was a Set or an alien. It was thousands of years old, and that was enough for the moment. Seemingly, she was already sufficiently committed to the alien hypothesis not to demand final proof. That's the legal mind for you.

"Gley found the skull," I said. "He deserves credit for the discovery. When you come to write it up in the history book, don't forget that, will you?"

Mentally, I added, *But even if you do, we won't.* At heart, I'm a sentimentalist. I wanted to think that Gley could get something out of his obsession. Stubbornness is entitled to its reward.

"You brought this back from inside the mountain?" she asked.

"That's right," I said.

"And Johann's still down there?"

I wasn't impressed by the switch to first names. "That's right," I said again. "Alone. Pursuing his Orphean quest through the terrible underworld, despite earthquakes and monsters. Quite a hero. And who knows what he might not find to startle the sunlit world?"

"He's dead," she opined.

"In a manner of speaking," I admitted. "But his name will live on. He'll become a kind of folk hero, won't he? The man who discovered that the world was once the property of another kind. The man who made the discovery which showed incontrovertibly that somewhere in the galaxy, probably not too far away, there is a race more advanced than man. A race with power over their own biological destiny such as we have only dreamed of. And who—presumably—have spent the last few thousand years exploiting that power in lieu of becoming champion colonists of our galactic arm."

I was fishing for some kind of opinion—some glimpse of what the notion might mean to her beyond the immediate political implications for Geb and its masters. But judges fall into the habit of keeping their inner visions very much to themselves. All that spills from their lips is a never-ending stream of legal niceties, technical observations and the occasional summing up. In this instance she wasn't even going to sum up.

"We'll have to establish a proper base here," she said. "There will have to be a proper excavation, even if we're unlikely to find anything useful at all. Even if the odds are millions to one against . . . if there *is* something to be found we must find it."

"The lure of alien artifacts?" I commented, ironically.

"Stop it, Alex," said Linda, wearily. "There's no need for it."

I stopped it. There was, indeed, no need for it.

"Do you want some coffee?" I said, in a different tone of voice. "I'll get some wood to build up the fire a bit."

As I turned away toward the door I reached out and picked up the skull. To Helene Levasseur I said, "I'd like to keep this, if you have no objection. The people who sent us out here will want to see it. And its significance extends far beyond this one world. You do see that, don't you?"

The gray-haired woman debated the point mentally for a few seconds. The brevity of the debate probably didn't do justice to the struggle of impulses. She answered in the affirmative. I put the skull down again, having established my claim. I left Linda and Mme. Levasseur together, feeling that they might find one another more congenial company than either of them would—for the time being, at least—find me.

Out on the verandah I paused, leaning over the rail to feel the cold air of the early breeze on my face. I looked up into the cloudless sky.

And up, and up, and up. . . .

❦ Epilogue ❦

It was, at least, an experiment of sorts. I didn't really
hold out much hope that the beginning would be follow.

The cameras followed Niccolo Pietrasante as he left the
floor of the United Nations. The microphones picked up
the waves of applause surging unsteadily across the audi-
torium. As Pietrasante disappeared from view the director
began to cut quickly from one camera to another as they
picked up particular delegates, to see whether or not they
joined in with the applause and how enthusiastically. The
wave died down slowly, but the cameras had no time to
check more than a dozen of the delegates likely to take
some further part in the debate.

In the hotel room the relaxation of tension was obvious. The most nervous of the four—the man named
Alexis Alexander—came to his feet, as if he needed to
move and to act in order to discharge some of the static
energy which had built up inside him. The girl, whose
name was Mariel Valory, let herself sink back into the
softness of her armchair. The other two, seemingly less
affected by the end of the speech, retained their positions
and betrayed their change of state only by slight movements of the hands and features. One was a tall blonde
woman named Karen Karelia, the other was Peter
Alexander, son of the older man.

"Do you want a drink?" asked the elder Alexander of
his son. He had already poured three, but was hesitating
before the fourth glass.

"Celebrating already?" asked Peter, by way of reply.

"Not exactly. Do you want one or not?"

"No thanks. I have to be going soon."

Alex replaced the screw-cap on the bottle carefully.
The tension that had attended Pietrasante's speech was al-

most gone, but the other tension was still there. The younger man was not only making no attempt to mute or mask his hostility but was, indeed, making something of a fetish out of it. He had not expected the reunion to be easy—after all, he had been away for more than five years—but he had looked forward to some kind of show, however false. Peter was a still a neo-Christian, still a one-worlder, still as firmly committed as ever to the dogma that man's one and only priority was the Earth and the making of a just society which would bring forth a new and healthy human consciousness that would have no need of far stars and colonies and other such evidences of fear, frustration and power-fantasy.

Alex handed drinks to Mariel and Karen, and then recovered his own from the sideboard. He sat down next to his son.

"You don't have to go yet," he said. "You've hardly said anything."

"What is there to say?" retorted the younger man. "The only things we have to talk over are being debated on the TV. And even that's a fake. The real decisions have all been taken—in secret. *That*'s just a performance. And so is this, isn't it?"

"No more than the rest of life is a performance," replied Alex.

"Do you want us to go?" asked Karen.

Her question was addressed to the older but it was the other who answered: "No. Stay. My father wanted me to meet you . . . or was it you to meet me?"

"And now we have," said the woman. "So perhaps we ought to go, and give you some privacy."

"It's not necessary," Peter assured her. "We have nothing private to discuss—and any public discussion is likely to be sterile. Everything's settled already. Just like . . ." He nodded toward the TV set.

"We haven't got forever to play this game," retorted Karen, her temper giving way just a little. "Alex isn't going to be on Earth for more than a couple of months, and for much of that you won't be able to see him. I suppose he *did* tell you?"

She glanced at Alex, giving the impression that she was annoyed with him rather than with the younger man.

"I told him," confirmed Alex.

"Is that why you're so bitter?" asked the woman of the boy.

"Hardly," said Peter. "It didn't come as a surprise. I take it that the two of you are likely to be going with him on the new expedition?"

"Probably," contributed Mariel.

"More worlds to save. More colonies to snatch back from the jaws of disaster."

"Actually," said Alex, "no. This time it's a different kind of mission. Exploratory."

Peter waited for him to amplify, but he said nothing more. Neither of the two women volunteered to add anything.

"Security," said the young man. "You can't say any more than that. Maybe not even that much. And I won't be able to see you once you begin preparations for the mission. I'm surprised they let you see me at all. I must be an embarrassment to you. A starman whose son is a neo-Christian minister. But we still aren't quite an illegal organization?"

"Rather the reverse, isn't it?" put in the girl. "My impression is that the Church has become familiar and well-established. It's lost its revolutionary aspect—at least in the eyes of the public."

The young man met her gaze. A slight shadow passed across his face. He wasn't angry—several years of emotional training had just about eliminated anger from his repertoire of reactions, converting it into sullen resentment or frustration.

"We were never seen as revolutionary," he answered. "We're pacifists, and no one sees pacifism as dangerous in this day and age. It's just a kind of vulgar joke. We're too easy to kill to be regarded as dangerous. People don't realize how revolutionary that is—the willingness to die rather than capitulate to violence."

"But you never managed to eradicate violence, did you? Or even call it into question in the way your founders envisaged. You never made the man in the street think twice about the gun in his pocket. Apart from your own recruits, that is."

"We've introduced *some* doubt into his mind," said Peter. "It's a matter of keeping it there, and making it grow."

"It's the people who admit the seed of doubt that are most likely to get killed," said Karen. "Everyone knows that your crowd are crazy—you'll happily let yourselves get trampled and so there's no point. It's the people who are still hesitating that are at risk, neither one thing nor the other. And the successes you win depend on the other guy's ability to recognize you for what you are. Try it on a man who doesn't know—or even one who doesn't care—and you get your head blown off right along with the next one. Isn't that right, Alex?"

The older man was silent for a moment, remembering something that had happened a long time ago, and which now seemed very remote indeed.

"I never had anything against that part of it," he said, eventually. "That always seemed to make a kind of sense, albeit a hopeful kind. There always did seem to be a sort of freedom in the refusal to capitulate to force. And no snide comment about the freedom to get your head blown off affects that fact. If someone tries to push you and can't be prevented then the only freedom you have left is the freedom to refuse any measure of cooperation whatever. It may only amount to the freedom to be hurt, but it's worth *something*. As a philosophy of life it lacks flexibility, but when it really comes down to it . . . but the rest of it is wrong. The one-world dogma."

"That's the issue which raises the stronger feelings," conceded Peter. "And why not? When there are people all over the world lacking food, lacking shelter, lacking work, with fear and pain omnipresent, then it's bound to raise strong feelings when the UN decides that *their* problems don't matter, that *they* can't be helped, because the important thing is to recreate the whole sorry situation elsewhere . . . time after time after time . . . more worlds for the chosen people to use for themselves . . . more worlds where the chosen people can generate their own poor and desperate, their own underprivileged. And people like you won't rest until we've created poverty and hardship all over the universe."

There was a brief silence following the end of the speech. Then Mariel Valory answered. She said, "And what about people like you? Suppose you remake the world according to the image you desire . . . what then? Do *you* rest? Or can you commit yourself so powerfully only because you believe along with your opponents that your task is impossible?"

"If we remade Earth the way it *can* be remade," said Peter, "then we wouldn't need to go to the stars. We wouldn't be cursed with the acquisitive compulsion that drives us to find new things and pollute them. And there's no need to give me the old argument about acquisitiveness being necessary to human well-being because once we have no more goals to strive for we're no better than stagnating vegetables. I've heard it before. There are other goals, apart from blind acquisitiveness and rapaciousness. All the *real* goals are inside us, not outside. Not even if we go to the ends of the universe. It's what's inside us that matters, where we can go and what we can do in our minds and our hearts."

"And where *can* we go?" asked Mariel, quietly.

The young man didn't answer. Instead, he said, "You've been to the colonies. You've seen what kind of people are there, and what they're doing. I haven't, and you can't tell me what you found because except for the official version that fat politician just gave to the UN and the TV-parasites of the world-at-large it's secret. But can you look me straight in the eye and say I'm wrong when I talk about acquisitiveness and rapaciousness?"

She did look him straight in the eye, but she said, "No. And I don't have to. We accept that. It's you that won't."

The young man's face did not change. He merely looked away, back toward his father.

"Forget it," said Alexis Alexander. "This isn't what we're here for. You're right—the argument's being fought out behind the TV screen. What matters to us is where we fit in—with one another as well as with all that. I've been away for five years. I'm soon going to be away for *more* years . . . how many I can't tell. Can't we just for a moment set all the arguments aside and meet on common ground?"

It was impossible to tell whether the appeal reached the younger man or not. When he spoke, it was to say, "Where did you get those scars?"

The older man touched his face reflexively. "Dendra," he said. "Something like a big cat. It was several days before I could get back to the ship, by which time it had partly healed up and was healing up as best it could. It was too late to make a clean repair without plastic surgery. I could get them removed now, but. . . ."

"But you rather like them."

"But I don't know when I can find the time."

"So you'll take them exploring. They'll help your image. I suppose you can't tell me what you're exploring *for*?"

"I don't know. Not now, though they might unfreeze the word before we actually set out. Mariel and Karen will probably be going with me. And one or two more, appointed by the UN. Not Nathan Parrick—he's got his own ambitions here on Earth. Some other UN personnel. But I can't tell you where we're going. Someday. . . ."

"Someday you can write a book about it," said Peter. "When you're old and it doesn't matter any more. Or someone will ghost it for you because you can't even grip a pen or push the button on a dictaphone."

"Maybe," said the older man.

"What's the ship going to be called?" asked Peter. "The *Icarus*, maybe?"

"I don't know. It's not for me to choose."

The younger man seemed to be much more sure of himself in talking to his father than he had been in talking to the girl. It was, in fact, much easier. All he had to do was resist.

Now he sighed. "I think I'd better go," he said. "I don't think there's any common ground left where we can meet. There was none when I saw you five years ago, when I was seventeen and you were about to lift off for the stars. We're worlds apart even while we're both on Earth. My life is here but yours, no matter where your feet are resting, is anywhere but. We were only connected in the first place by an accident of heredity, and it's a long time now since my mother died. You were halfway across the world even then—lost in some carefully-preserved wilderness so we couldn't even reach you with a call for help. That's where you always will be. I suppose some might argue that *somebody* has to be out in the wilderness, but I don't see that. I never have. So much for heredity."

Then he left.

Alexis Alexander stood up and watched the door close. Then he went to the side table to refill his glass. When he turned again to face his companions his face was expressionless.

"Not a great success," he commented.

Neither of the women bothered to signal their agreement.

"I wanted to tell him what we'll be looking for," he went on. "I wanted to tell him that we found traces of someone else . . . footprints on Crusoe's island. I wanted to tell him that maybe *they'd* turned to thinking his way, deciding that one world is enough and turning their attention to developing themselves, finding new goals in their minds and hearts. But I couldn't. Not just because it's secret but because he wouldn't have understood. He couldn't. What he means by seeking goals within oneself means anything but biological engineering. He still sees human nature as something God-given and Christ-perfected. He wants us all to be what one man twenty-three centuries ago told us that we can and ought to be. Even unto the crucifixion."

"There's nothing you could ever say or do," said Mariel. "He's right when he says that you're worlds apart. He's right when he says that the accident of heredity no longer signifies any kind of connection between you."

"Sure," said Alex. "I know that. I'm irredeemable. Even he's given up on me."

"He's entitled to go his own way," said Karen. "And so are we."

"No matter how hard I try," the man said, in a distant voice that was already recovering its customary note of whimsical sobriety, "I can't shake the notion that in the final analysis *all* of this . . . Earth, the star-worlds, the Sets and their makers, and everything that may yet be there for us to find . . . all of this might be a kind of cosmic joke. When all is said and done we might just be another evolutionary dead end. And God might be a giant squid."

"You can shake it," Karen assured him dryly. "If you really wanted to. All you have to do is try."